SUMMIT OF SEDUCTION

The Springs—Eight

ELENA AITKEN

Chapter One

THERE WERE a million other places Cynthia Giles should be.
Well, maybe not a million. But there were definitely a few other
places she could think of that would be more appropriate for
her to be on Valentine's Day night besides riding in a pickup
truck, only a bump and jostle away from bouncing into Seth
McBride, who sat only inches away from her. Inches.

Too close.

Way too close. Especially considering every nerve in her
body was totally aware of his proximity and was going
completely haywire because of it. Sure, she'd been in close
spaces with Seth before. Very close. But that was different. Her
body should not be betraying her with its obvious and totally
uncontrollable attraction to him. Even if he was incredibly
handsome in that rugged mountain man, outdoorsy way. If
that was your kind of thing. And it was most certainly not her
kind of thing. At least it hadn't been.

Cynthia risked a glance over at him. One hand rested casually on the steering wheel as he navigated the truck through the
snowy roads as if he'd done it a thousand times, which he

probably had. A lock of his hair flopped over his eye. He swiped it away, and in doing so, caught her looking at him.

"If you want me to drop you somewhere, I can," he said. "You don't have to come with me."

It was the second time he'd tested her, trying to give her an out. From the moment he'd set foot in her shop, the Store Room, he'd been testing her, almost as if he'd been trying to get her to admit something she wouldn't. But what? It was Valentine's Day. It was bad enough that she didn't have a date. She didn't have to admit it to him. Not Seth McBride. Not after what they'd….

"No," she said quickly, and returned her gaze straight ahead out the windshield to the snow that started to come down harder. "I told you I'd come to check on the puppies, and I will."

Less than an hour ago, he'd come into her store to buy dog kibble for a stray husky who'd found her way into the maintenance shed at Stone Summit, the local ski hill where he was general manager, and had a litter of puppies. Or at least that was the story he told her. Not that he had any reason to lie. Why would he?

To get her to spend Valentine's Day with him, a little voice in the back of her head said.

She quickly dismissed it. Seth wasn't the type of guy to go to such lengths to get a girl to spend time with him. Hell, he wasn't the type of guy to go to any lengths. He was the type of guy who worked his way through women like consumables. It was well known around town that Seth McBride didn't *do* relationships. He did one-night stands and casual flings, but that was it. She herself had known it for years; even if she did have a momentary lapse of judgment—twice—and thought maybe, just maybe it could be different with her…that moment was over.

"If you insist." There was a hint of humor in his voice and she whipped around in her seat.

"I don't insist." How the hell did he do that? Turn it into her idea? It was Seth who had walked into her store and told her about the puppies. It was Seth who asked her if she wanted to come see them. "You're the one who..." She trailed off at his grin. He was trying to get her riled up. And it worked.

Cynthia crossed her arms and faced forward again. "Why do you do that?"

"What?"

"Like to get me worked up."

"Because you're incredibly sexy when you're mad." Seth spoke the words so simply it took her off guard. She risked another glance at him but he was focused on driving as he turned down the short road that led to Stone Summit, the newly reopened ski hill that Malcolm Stone owned and Seth managed. A job that was set to become even busier now that Malcolm's girlfriend, Cynthia's best friend, Kylie Wilson, was getting ready to leave town to go to school in Vancouver. Malcolm planned to split his time between Vancouver and the ski hill, which would leave Seth primarily in charge. *A role that would no doubt go to his head even more*, Cynthia thought with a sniff.

She couldn't explain why she was so antagonistic toward the man. Okay, she could. She just didn't want to. It was a proven fact that Seth was a womanizer and she hated herself for her moment of weakness and falling for his charms. Not once, but twice. She was not that girl. Sure, Cynthia liked to have a good time. She liked to enjoy herself and no one appreciated a party more than she did. But after a failed attempt at a relationship with Jax Carver, the head chef at the Springs, she'd sworn off men. Or more specifically, men who weren't interested in something serious. And it was clear Seth wasn't interested. But he didn't have to be such an ass about it.

"I'm sorry," Seth said, taking her off guard.

For a second, she thought maybe he was finally going to apologize for the way he'd gotten what he wanted from her and then quickly moved on to the next woman in line. She raised her eyebrow and waited for him to say more.

"I didn't mean to make you mad." He grinned and she hated the way her body responded to him while at the same time she wanted to smack the smile off his face.

She shook her head. Only a few weeks ago, Cynthia had thought things could be different between them, that maybe the connection they shared physically was enough to actually turn into something more. Because, damn, even if she didn't want to admit it, there was definitely a physical connection between them. She'd actually been naive enough to think that maybe the right guy for her had been under her nose all along, disguised as Seth McBride. But then she'd discovered his true colors when she caught him having dinner at the Stillwater Grill with some other woman. She hadn't even seen her face, nor had she bothered to confront him about it. Why would she? It's not as if they were dating. Besides, she'd known that was how Seth was right from the start. It shouldn't have come as a surprise. Her anger was her shield, and she'd carry it as long as it took for her to forget the way his touch made her feel, the way his kiss made her come alive.

"Hey." Seth grabbed her arm, forcing her to turn and face him. "I *am* sorry, Cyn. Really."

The light was too dark for her to read his eyes to see whether he was being sincere, but there was something in his voice that she believed and she let some of her hostility melt away. After all, even if there was nothing between them, spending the night visiting newborn puppies certainly beat the alternative, which was sitting home alone and drinking a bottle of wine by herself on Valentine's Day. And he did say she looked sexy. She forced herself not to smile.

4

"How many puppies did you say there were?"

He grinned; his teeth flashed in the dim light of the truck. "Three."

She nodded. "Right."

Seth looked at her a moment longer and held her eyes for just a fraction of a second before he turned back to the road. She turned her head again and mentally chastised herself. *Get it together, Cynthia. He's just a guy. Just a guy.*

She could tell herself that all she wanted, but it was a lie and she damn well knew it. Seth McBride was more than a guy.

"Here we are."

Cynthia snapped to attention as Seth pulled up next to the steel building that she knew housed the snow groomers and snowmobiles for the ski hill. She'd never actually been in the maintenance shed—why would she? But she'd spent enough time at Stone Summit to know most of the buildings.

After Seth hopped out of the truck, she waited for a moment to see whether he'd come around and open her door. He didn't. Not that she expected him to. It's not as though they were on a date or anything. *Still.* With a sigh, Cynthia opened the door and turned to slide out into the chilly night.

"Here." To her surprise, Seth held his hand out for her. "Let me help you."

It took her a second to realize what he was offering. She looked at his hand and then back at him. "I got it." With a less than glamorous move, Cynthia hopped down from the cab of the truck. When she saw the look on his face, she instantly regretted not accepting his help. Before she could say or do anything, he turned away and went to retrieve the bag of kibble from the back.

"They're right in here." Seth gestured with his head and Cynthia followed as he led the way into the shed.

They dodged and weaved their way past equipment and

workbenches; the smell of oil and something else, something distinctly male, hung in the air. She'd never been in such a space before. It felt oddly as if she were trespassing into some other world. Seth's world. She watched him, matching his steps, being sure to avoid the bits of machinery that stuck out until they reached the far corner of the shed.

"You put her way in the back?"

Seth shrugged casually. "Don't blame me." He gave her that sly smile again. "She chose the spot. I just went with it. Stubborn female and all that." He winked and looked away.

Cynthia shook her head and looked around him. "Is that her, over there?"

"Just in the corner. Maybe be careful before you get too close to her pups." He put a hand on her arm to still her. Cynthia froze, but not because of the action. More from the electricity that flew through her from one simple touch. Even through her winter jacket, his touch had a powerful effect on her. She had to turn away, unable to look him in the eye. "I don't know how she'll react, Cyn. I wouldn't want you to—"

"What?"

When he didn't answer, she turned and their eyes locked. For a moment, she thought she saw something else in his dark brown eyes, but then he blinked and the moment was gone. "I don't know the dog," he said quickly. "And you never know how a new mom will react. Let alone a stray. Just be careful."

She slipped past him and moved toward the box in the corner. "Don't worry, I'll—" Her words dropped away when she saw the beautiful husky with three impossibly tiny little puppies tucked up next to her. The dog lifted her head and looked at her with big, sorrowful eyes. Cynthia dropped to her knees on the concrete and reached her hand out to the dog, who sniffed it once before she licked it and tilted her head into Cynthia's hand to be stroked. Of course, Cynthia obliged.

"She likes you." Seth was next to her, on his knees on the

concrete and for once, Cynthia's stomach didn't flip or react at his proximity. Instead, all her energy was focused on the dog.

"What's her name?"

"I told you, she's a stray. She wandered in here earlier tonight and—"

"I know, but she needs a name. She's a mama now. It seems wrong to keep calling her *the dog*." Cynthia scratched the dog's ears for another second before the dog bent her head to attend to her puppies. She licked them all in turn and nuzzled them closer to her belly. "She's beautiful and look how much she loves her babies." Cynthia's heart swelled. She'd always had a soft spot when it came to animals, although somehow she'd never had a pet of her own. When she was younger, her mother was so busy working that she refused to take on the responsibility of another life; even though Cynthia would beg her and try to convince her that she'd do all the work, it hadn't worked. As she got older, it was easy to see that her mother might have been right. Besides, she was too busy being a teenager and getting into trouble; a pet was the last thing from her mind. By the time she was old enough to really think about it again, her mother had been diagnosed with breast cancer and she'd had her hands full of taking care of her and the store.

"What are you thinking?"

Cynthia's smile was sad, but she answered Seth honestly. "I was just thinking how much I missed by never having a pet."

"You've never had a dog?"

She shook her head.

"Or a cat?"

She shook her head again.

"Well then, I think you should name her."

She turned her head to see Seth only inches away from her. He was close enough to kiss and for a moment she let herself entertain the idea. But only for a moment. She looked back at

7

the dog. "The fact that I've never had a pet hardly makes me qualified to name her."

"It makes you perfectly qualified." His voice was low and sexy and she knew without looking that he stared at her. With renewed determination, she kept her gaze fixed on the dog.

"Okay…" She pondered her options but there was only one that spoke to her. "Nala."

"Nala?"

"It means loved." Cynthia reached out and stroked the dog's soft fur. "And I think she definitely loves and is loved." The puppies wriggled and made soft mewling sounds until Nala tended to them and nudged them gently with her muzzle. "Yes." Unbidden tears pricked at her eyes and she blinked hastily to keep them at bay.

Silently, Seth moved around behind her and wrapped his arm around her. She didn't slide away the way she should have and when he pulled her in to his chest, instead of stopping him, she leaned into his solid muscle. He was strong and warm and smelled of fresh cut wood and something else that was uniquely Seth. She closed her eyes against the unexpected emotion the dog and her puppies brought on and let herself have the moment in Seth's arm. Because that's all it would be.

Just a moment.

DAMN.

She felt good in his arms.

He had no claim on her, no reason to reach out and hold her. In fact, Seth had half-expected Cynthia to pull away and put that ever present distance between them again. But the moment he saw the tears in her eyes, he'd acted totally on instinct. There was no way he was going to sit by and watch her get emotional. Not that it meant anything, he told himself.

He would have done the same for any woman. He simply could not handle it when women cried or got upset.

Especially Cynthia.

He shut down the thought. Besides a few hookups—a few hookups that had been nothing short of freaking amazing—they had nothing. They were friends. And even then, they hardly seemed like friends these days. For a while, Seth thought that maybe there could be something between the two of them. He'd never felt that way about another woman before. After all, his entire MO was to have fun and get out before it got serious. Growing up with just his dad and his string of girlfriends after his mom died, it was easy for him to swear off serious relationships.

Things with Cynthia felt different, but then, just when he started to consider something more than just a casual fling, she pulled away. He couldn't explain it, but she stopped answering his calls, and made a point to ignore him when they ran into each other. He'd never pretended to understand women, but Cynthia was in a class of confusing all on her own.

It didn't matter anyway, because really, they had nothing in common besides a few joint friends. Besides, she'd made it clear that she didn't want anything further to do with him. He should have been smart enough to leave her alone.

But he couldn't.

Something about the damn woman kept him coming back. Had him seeking her out. Just the way he had earlier tonight. It was Valentine's Day. She should have had a date and even though she said she did, he knew she didn't. Not that he could understand it. With her long, lean body with curves in all the right places, and the fiery red hair that he knew for damn sure was natural, the woman was smoking hot. There was no reason she shouldn't have had a date.

Unless…

No. He wasn't going to put any more thought into it. For

9

the moment, she was in his arms and she felt damn good. That was good enough for him.

"What's wrong?" He whispered into her ear, close enough to kiss her earlobe. An urge he fought. "Are you okay?"

She nodded against his chest. "I'm fine. I just...I don't know. It's just so sweet watching her. The immediate love and instinct she has for her babies." She turned in his arms so their noses almost touched. He could feel her soft breath on his face. "Do you think every mom feels that way?"

Again, he fought the urge to kiss her, knowing she'd just pull away and the moment would be lost. "I do. I've seen a lot of animals with their babies, and I've yet to see any mother who didn't react just the way Nala has."

Her smile was gorgeous and even in the dim maintenance shed, it lit up her face. "Nala," she repeated. "Do you like the name?"

"It's perfect."

Their eyes locked and Seth moved his hand up her back and brushed her hair off the back of her neck. Forget every reason he shouldn't. No matter what it was Cynthia thought she was running from, it felt right being with her. He closed the slight gap between them and brushed her lips with his. They were soft and slightly chilled from the cool air, but after a moment she opened to him in a soft, slow kiss. His body responded at once with the promise of what was to come. Gently, he pulled her to her feet without leaving her mouth and pulled her even closer until their bodies were pressed together.

Just as he began to think it might be a good Valentine's Day after all, Cynthia stepped back and broke their kiss.

Damn her pushing him away again.

"Cynthia, why are you—"

"I don't think...No." Her hand went to her mouth and she shook her head. "I should probably get going."

"You don't have to go." He reached for her again. "We have such a good time together."

Something flashed across her face and then the confusion was gone, replaced by a hardness as she closed herself off again. "We did," she said. "Once."

"Twice."

Her eyes flashed and she took a deep breath. "I have…I have a date."

He opened his mouth to call her bluff. When he'd walked into the Store Room to pick up the bag of kibble, she'd said something about a date for Valentine's Day but he hadn't believed her. Or had he just not wanted to believe her?

"With who?" He hated that he probably came off as a jealous boyfriend; that wasn't his style. Not even a little. He didn't care. Except when it came to the woman in front of him, he did. And it made him crazy.

She looked at him then and stared right into his soul with those striking jade green eyes. "It's none of your business, Seth McBride."

You had your chance. She didn't say it, but she might as well have for the way she looked at him and crossed her arms over her chest, shutting him out.

Seth shook his head, ran a hand through his hair and gave her his best shit-eating grin. "Well, I wouldn't want you to be late for Mr. Wonderful." It was easier to be an ass than try to get to the bottom of whatever it was that was going on with her. Besides, if she didn't want him, plenty of women would.

He stalked off through the shed, not waiting for her to follow but knowing she would.

Chapter Two

"I WISH you didn't have to go."

Cynthia sat among piles of clothes on her best friend Kylie's bed while her friend sorted and packed around her. Instead of helping, the way she'd said she would, she'd so far spent the time trying to figure out a way to get Kylie to stay. It hadn't worked.

"Please don't, Cyn." Kylie took a scarf from her hands and shoved it in a bag. "You know I don't want to leave. Please don't make it any harder."

Cynthia sat up straight. It was true. She should be more supportive. She knew she should and she would be, too, if it wasn't so damn hard to watch her best friend leave right when Cynthia needed her the most. Okay, she didn't really need Kylie any more than usual but losing your best and really, closest friend was a hard pill to swallow.

"I know," Cynthia said. "I'm sorry. I'll be more supportive. No," she corrected herself. "I *am* supportive. You know how proud I am of you going off to nursing school all on your own. That's huge. More than huge. You're so brave and I'm so proud of you for following your passion. I really am." Tears welled up in her eyes, and to cover it, she busied herself folding a sweater. She really needed to stop crying so much. It was getting annoying.

"You're not getting teary, are you?" Kylie teased, but they both knew there would be plenty of tears from both of them when Kylie actually made the final move to Vancouver and away from Cedar Springs in the next few weeks. Kylie bent down and tried to look at Cynthia's face. "Cyn, you're not crying, are you? For real, don't cry right now. I can't handle it if you start crying. You're not the crier."

Cynthia sniffed hard. The tears she tried so hard to hold back fell onto the pile of clothes below. "I know." She swiped at her face. "I'm not a crier. I don't know what's wrong with me lately. First it was the puppies last night and now this, and it's not like you're even leaving today or anything. I mean, I don't need to get sad yet, right? I should just—"

"Wait. What puppies?"

"What?" Cynthia sniffed hard again and wiped her nose.

"Puppies." Kylie eyed her strangely. "What puppies?"

Cynthia racked her brain, quickly trying to figure out something she could say that wouldn't be a lie, but also wouldn't be the truth. She couldn't explain it but she didn't want Kylie to know she'd hooked up with Seth. It's not as if she was ashamed or anything. Well, okay. She was a little ashamed. But only when it became clear that she wasn't anything more than a random hookup to him.

She shook her head to clear it of images of Seth: His arms. His hard chest. His lips on hers.

"Cyn. Hello, earth to Cynthia."

She blinked hard and focused on her friend, who now directly in front of her, heedless of the pile of clothes she was messing up. "Are you okay?"

Cynthia nodded. "I'm fine. Why?"

"I've been talking to you for the last few minutes and you still haven't answered my question."

"What question?"

The look that Kylie gave her helped Cynthia snap back into the present. "The puppies?"

"Right. Seth took me to see some puppies that were born up at Stone Summit yesterday. You should get Malcolm to show you before you go. They're so cute. Really, the cutest little things ever and their mama is—"

"Seth?"

Cynthia blinked hard. She might as well just get it over with. "Yes, Seth. The puppies are in the maintenance shed so naturally he knew about it."

"Naturally."

Cynthia didn't like the way her friend looked at her. She knew Kylie suspected something was up between her and Seth, but she didn't want Kylie to know the truth. At first she just hadn't told Kylie about their hookup because that was after the big New Year's party when Kylie and Malcolm were having a major fight or crisis or whatever, and then when it happened again, she hadn't said anything because she didn't want Kylie to say anything to Malcolm and have him say something to Seth and then...well, then it didn't matter because whatever was happening between them stopped happening. So really, there was no point in mentioning the past. Especially because it was Seth. And Kylie would just shake her head and say something like *but that's what Seth does.* And she didn't need to hear that. Not now.

"Why did he show you last night? Were you on a date?"

"A date?" Cynthia almost choked. "Why would you say that?"

Kylie narrowed her eyes and gave her a look that told her she wasn't buying whatever Cynthia was trying to sell.

"Because it was Valentine's Day. Why else would you have been out with Seth last night?"

"It wasn't a date."

"But you told me you had a date."

Dammit. She had told Kylie that. At the time, she'd lied to her friend so she wouldn't feel sorry for her doing nothing on Valentine's Day when she herself was no doubt headed out for a romantic night. She'd told Seth the same lie. But that was different.

"I did," Cynthia said. "Well, sort of. It wasn't really a date so much as...I was working." She dropped her arms next to her side. It was just easier to come clean. "I sort of had a date with the store and then my mom and a glass of wine."

"Oh, Cyn." Kylie rubbed her arm and although the action was no doubt designed to make her feel better, it just made her feel guilty for lying to her best friend.

She jerked away from her friend's touch and grabbed a pair of leggings from another pile. "You aren't seriously packing these, are you? Because they look way better on me."

Kylie tipped her head and gave it a shake. Cynthia hoped her eyes were telling Kylie to back off. She should know her well enough to know when she didn't want to talk. Kylie grabbed the leggings from her hands.

"Look." Cynthia jumped up from the bed and paced over to the closet, which was mostly bare. "Just because I didn't have a date for Valentine's Day doesn't mean you need to feel sorry for me. I'm perfectly fine on my own. I don't need a man."

"It's not about *needing* a man, Cyn."

She knew it. It wasn't about that. She took a deep breath but didn't turn around.

"So tell me about the puppies."

Cynthia turned around and waited a beat before she answered her friend. She knew what Kylie really wanted to know. She put a smile on her face. "They are *so* cute, Kylie.

They're only about this big." She held her hands slightly apart. "And the mama is so sweet and loves her babies so much, you can just see it. It's amazing how animals just instinctively love their babies. Like one minute, it was just her. And the next, she had three little ones to take care of. Can you imagine?"

Kylie shook her head slowly and a smile crept across her face.

"What?"

"It's nothing," Kylie said. "But I've never seen you like this. So passionate about something. It's…it's pretty cool. So do they have names?"

"Well…sort of. I mean, the mama does. Seth asked me to name her."

"Seth did?"

Cynthia was so wrapped up in her story, she ignored the little unasked question in Kylie's voice. She needed to stop trying to turn her relationship, or whatever it was, with Seth into something it wasn't. Because it wasn't anything. "He did," she said simply. "So I named her Nala. It means 'loved' because she was clearly so loved by her babies and there was so much love from her. It was…what?" Kylie looked at her with that look on her face that she knew too well. "Stop it." Cynthia tossed a t-shirt in her direction. "Just pack."

Kylie took the t-shirt and shoved it in a duffle bag. "I think it's nice that you've been spending time with Seth."

"I haven't," Cynthia lied.

"But you said—"

"I said he showed me the puppies in the maintenance shed. That was it."

"But, I just thought—"

"You thought wrong." Cynthia tossed another t-shirt in her friend's direction and headed for the door. "Look, can we talk more later? I should get to the store and check in."

"Of course." Kylie looked as if she might say more, but

to Cynthia's relief, she didn't. She gave Kylie a quick hug and left her in her tiny apartment, surrounded by piles of clothes. She should have stayed and helped her finish packing; she knew she should have. It's what a good friend would have done, but she needed space from Kylie's questions. They were hitting too close to home and for the life of her, Cynthia couldn't figure out why she couldn't even tell her best friend the truth about what was going on with her and Seth.

Probably because she had no idea.

IT HAD BEEN a long day on the ski hill. Not that any day on the slopes of Stone Summit was a long, hard day. Not by any stretch. Seth knew how lucky he was to be able to do what he loved for a living. Still, there were some days when even skiing felt more like work than play. Fortunately, those days were few and far between. But as he reached behind his back and used his poles to click out of his bindings, even Seth had to admit a bad day working at a ski hill was still a pretty damn good day.

The Silver chair had gone down, which meant a ton of unhappy customers who were waiting in line for a chair that wasn't going to be working any time soon. And of course, as the hill manager, he was the guy who had to break the bad news and hand out vouchers to ski another day for the really upset customers. Fortunately, that was only a handful of the people. The vast majority of people Seth got to deal with were happy to be out in the fresh air, once again enjoying the local ski hill.

Those people and his own good memories of skiing were a large part of the reason Seth had jumped at the chance to manage the newly reopened ski hill in Cedar Springs. That and he'd been floating from job to job without any real direction. Just like his love life. But he was getting older and that life-style had started to lose a bit of the luster it once held.

Either way, working with Malcolm Stone, helping him with the setup of Stone Summit, had been a perfect fit and Seth was in his element. He owed a lot to Malcolm, who'd taken a risk to hire him. Malcolm had done an amazing thing by reopening the hill. Sure, it was a smart business move, especially with the exclusive Springs resort new to town as well, but Seth knew it was about more than business for Malcolm. Stone Summit had been a passion project for Malcolm, and had more to do with the woman he loved than anything else.

For Seth, that was a hard concept to wrap his head around. He'd never been in love like that. Never had he been willing to change his entire life for a woman. An image of a certain fiery redhead popped into his mind and he allowed himself to enter-tain the idea of Cynthia for a few moments. There was some-thing about that woman that he couldn't shake. She was like a drug that he couldn't get enough of. Too bad she didn't seem to feel the same way. It was clear that as far as Cynthia was concerned, nothing would ever happen between them. At least, nothing more.

Not that they'd ever planned for anything to happen in the first place. Hell, at the launch of Stone Summit on New Year's Eve, Cynthia had spent most of the night with some other guy. From the moment she'd stepped in the room, dancing and laughing, Seth couldn't take his eyes off her. Sure, he'd seen her before and even partied with her before, but there was something different about her that night. Soon they ended up dancing and that dancing turned into a few stolen kisses, which turned into sneaking off back to his apartment, and he knew he was in trouble. He never should have gone there. But it had been so damn good. One time hadn't been enough.

Even now, as he picked up his skis and carried them into the shed where he kept his equipment, his body remembered every second of being with her. The feel of her soft, creamy skin under his rough, work-worn hands. The way she responded so readily to every touch, every kiss. His dick twitched in his pants and Seth had to force himself to think of something else. It wasn't going to happen again.

Unless... No. There was no point torturing himself. Besides, there were plenty of women who did want to be with him. He'd never had to pursue a woman who clearly didn't want to be with him, and he wasn't about to start now.

Leaving his ski equipment, he unzipped his parka and walked through the shed. He needed to check on Nala and her pups. Nala. It was a great name. Of course Cynthia would give her the best name. He still couldn't believe she'd never had a pet. Maybe he'd give her one of the puppies?

"Nala. Hey, girl," he called through the shed, alerting the dog to his presence so he didn't spook her. "How are you doing?" He kept talking to her as he walked through the building. It was a habit he'd fallen easily into in the few days since she'd arrived. It was nice to have someone, or something, to talk to. If any of the guys heard him talking to the dog like that, he'd be ribbed for days.

"I brought you a—oh. Hi." Seth stopped short when he rounded the corner and saw Cynthia on the floor next to Nala's box. Just looking at her, with her long denim-clad legs tucked under her, her hair pulled back in a ponytail that he instinctively wanted to run his hands through and let fall around her shoulders, caused his groin to tighten. "I didn't expect you to be here."

She hopped up and dusted off her pants. "I'm sorry." She blushed. The color flooded her face and gave her a radiant glow that made her even more appealing. If it was possible. He loved that his presence never failed to cause her to blush. Not only was it incredibly erotic to see her react so hard and fast to him, it also told him everything he needed to know as far as how she really felt about him. Despite her protests. "I hope it's okay," she was saying. "I had some time before I had to be at the store and I thought I'd come check on our girl."

Our girl.

"It was cold last night and I wanted to make sure she had everything she needed and...I see you brought a space heater in." She pointed to the heater he'd hooked up in preparation for the temperature to drop. He'd tried to move Nala and her pups, maybe take them back to his place so he could watch them better, but his place wasn't really big enough. Besides that, the dog didn't seem to want to go anywhere and in the end, it just seemed easier to leave them in the maintenance shed and simply check on them.

"I did." He nodded dumbly and crossed his arms over his chest when what he really wanted to do was reach out and touch her. "I thought it might be good to keep her warm." *God, he sounded like an idiot.* He shook his head.

"It was a good idea."

"I have them sometimes." *Damn, he really was an idiot.* He didn't mean to sound like a total jackass.

"I'm sorry," Cynthia said quickly. "I wasn't implying...I'll go. I shouldn't have just—"

"No. You're fine. You can stay as long as you like. In fact, come whenever. I feel kind of like she's your dog, too." *Again, such an idiot. What was wrong with him?* "I mean, you named her, so...that kind of makes you involved. If you want to be, I mean."

He swallowed hard. He needed to stop talking. But if Cynthia thought he sounded stupid, she didn't show it. Instead, a beautiful smile crossed her face and lit up her features. "I'd like that."

Again, the urge to reach out and touch her was almost overwhelming, but she turned and dropped to her knees again, once again giving all her attention to the dogs. He watched her for a minute and used her distraction to compose himself. *What was it about the woman?*

He cleared his throat and squatted next to her. "How's our little mama doing today?" A strange look flashed across her face but it was gone so fast he couldn't be sure he saw it.

"She's so amazing." Cynthia's voice was soft and she stroked Nala's head as she spoke, almost as if she were encouraging the new mom. "It's just so incredible to see that maternal instinct. I just can't get over it."

"It's pretty crazy, isn't it?" He reached out and patted Nala as well, before he tentatively pet one of the pups with one finger. Nala watched him closely, but as if she sensed he wouldn't hurt her pups, she didn't object. "We should probably name these little guys, too, don't you think?"

"Oh, I can't do that. It was enough to name her. You should probably name the puppies. After all, they're yours."

Were they his? Just because Nala had come into his shed and he happened to be there, did that give him rights? Did he even want them? "Oh no. They're not mine. They're just hanging out here. I don't have pets." Hell, he couldn't even keep a plant alive. The last thing he needed was another living thing to be responsible for. "In fact, if you want them, you can—"

His phone rang, interrupting the thought, which was probably a good thing because Cynthia stared at him as if he were a monster. All because he said he didn't want them? He was only being realistic. What the hell was he going to do with a dog? Let alone a dog and her three pups. No, Nala could hang out until the puppies were old enough, but realistically, they couldn't stay with him after that.

He didn't bother excusing himself as he got up and pulled out his cell. *Malcolm.*

"Hey, what's up?"

"Where are you?"

"I'm in the shed with Cyn—the dogs." There was no point opening up that line of questioning with Malcolm. He didn't need to know about Cynthia. "Remember I told you about the puppies?"

"Right. Okay, well if you're done with puppy care, we need to go over the issue with the Silver chair. Can you meet me in my office in five?"

Seth agreed, hung up and waited a beat before he returned to Cynthia's side. "You can stay as long as you want with them," he said slowly. "And seriously, I mean it when I said you could come visit whenever. I'm not really the best caregiver and—"

"I think you've done a great job, Seth." She stood in front of him, and pulled her jacket tight around her body. "If it wasn't for you...well, Nala would be..." Tears filled her eyes again and instinctively, he reached out and took her hand.

"Hey." He squeezed gently. "It's okay. You don't have to cry. She's okay and the puppies are—"

"I know, I know." With her free hand, she wiped her eyes. "Honestly, I don't know what's wrong with me. I'm not usually so emotional. I think it's just everything with Kylie moving away. We've never been apart. I mean, not for any real amount of time and this is like...it's like losing a—" She cut herself off and pulled her hand away from his.

Instantly, Seth missed the connection.

"Wow." She looked away, but not before Seth caught the rosy glow on her cheeks. "I don't know why I'm sharing all that with you. It's not like you care or anything. I just—"

"It's okay." He reached for her hand again and she turned to look at him. "I do care," he said before he could stop himself. But it was true. Whatever was going on with Cynthia, upsetting her enough to make her cry, he found he really did care. "You can talk to me if you want. I'm a good listener. I have these two ears that work pretty good." He wiggled his ears, a childhood trick he'd mastered at the age of twelve, and she laughed.

Mission accomplished.

"Thanks for the offer," Cynthia said with a new smile on her face. "But I actually need to get going. Colton's been doing a good job at the store, but I can't leave him on his own forever or he will annihilate my potato chip supply."

"I'll walk you out."

She opened her mouth to agree, he assumed, but then closed it again and glanced at Nala and the puppies. "Actually, maybe I'll hang out for a few more minutes here before I get going. Is that okay?"

"Perfectly."

"I'll see you later?"

He nodded. "I certainly hope so." Before she could respond, he turned and walked through the shed, even though every fiber in his body ached to turn around and see the sexy blush that disappeared below the collar of her jacket. The blush that Seth knew without a doubt he'd put there.

Chapter Three

THE BLARING of her alarm burst through Cynthia's dream.
She shoved her head under her pillow, reached out blindly for
her snooze alarm and struggled in vain to get the dream back.
In it, she'd been lying in bed, the hard planes of an unseen
man's body behind her. A strong arm looped around her chest,
his hand flat against her belly as the man pulled her in tight so
she could feel exactly how excited he was to have her in bed
with him. His fingers trailed south to the cleft between her legs
while his lips found her neck and kissed the sensitive spot
behind her ear.

Cynthia moaned as he—

"Dammit." She rolled over as her alarm went off again
and the dream evaporated, this time for good. It was a varia-
tion of the same dream she'd had almost every night for the
last week. It always ended right before she was satisfied. Was it
telling her something? Probably. It had been way too long since
she'd had sex. Well…an image of Seth popped into her head.
Okay, it hadn't been that long. But she'd promised herself that
wouldn't happen again.

Although…

Not for the first time, Cynthia let herself entertain the idea of hooking up with him again. It wouldn't be the worst thing. As far as the sex went, it would definitely not be the worst thing. In fact, based on what she knew—and she definitely knew enough—it would be a damn good thing to have Seth McBride in her bed again.

No.

She dismissed the thought just the way she always did, before she could let it settle in. Sure, ever since he took her to introduce her to the puppies, she'd seen a different side of him. But it had only been a week and even though she was slowly discovering that there might be more to Seth McBride than she originally gave him credit for, it still wasn't a good idea to go there. The whole *fool me once* theory. Despite her past indiscretions, and no matter how frustrated her dreams were leaving her, Seth wasn't the answer.

As it turned out, she didn't have any more time to convince herself otherwise anyway. After the third time hitting her snooze alarm, there was no more putting it off. If she didn't get up and get in the shower in the next five minutes, there'd be no time for one at all and considering she'd played the same self-negotiation game the morning before, and had opted for the extra sleep, a shower was nonnegotiable.

With a sigh, she pulled the covers back and forced herself to step out onto the cold floor. *Damn, the furnace better not be on the fritz again.* She absolutely could not afford a repairman, not with the continual costs of her mother's meds and now Jess, the caregiver she'd hired to help alleviate some of her workload. Her mother's cancer was progressing quickly and since Linda was insistent on dying at home in her own bed, her care was becoming too much for Cynthia to handle on her own. As if that wasn't enough, the storefront desperately needed a coat of paint this spring. A detail she would have tried to cover up with some fresh flower planters if it hadn't been for a memo from the local Chamber of Commerce that encouraged all business owners in town to maintain their exteriors.

The memo was aimed at her. She knew it. Although everyone else in town was too polite to say anything outright, she knew the store needed a facelift and she'd make it a priority, too. Just as soon as she could find the money. And the energy.

Steam filled the small bathroom and when she stepped inside the shower, she let the hot water wash over her and warm her from the outside-in. Hopefully the water would wake her up. She'd been so tired lately that she'd even nodded off at the store the night before while she waited to close up.

She would have happily stayed in the shower all day, or at least until the hot water tank ran out but due to her little sleep-in, Cynthia was already running late. Jess would be there soon and Cynthia liked to check on her mom and have a moment to talk before Jess got there. Mornings were often some of her mother's best times; Cynthia didn't like to miss them.

There was no time to blow dry her long, thick hair, so she tugged it into a braid and quickly brushed her teeth, studying her reflection in the mirror as she did so.

What she saw wasn't good. Not at all. She looked worse than she felt. She must be coming down with something. In an effort to mask the exhaustion on her face, Cynthia took a minute to dab on some concealer under her eyes and swipe on some mascara. As an afterthought, she opened the medicine cabinet in search of some aspirin or even an old vitamin C tablet. Instead, her eyes locked on the box of tampons.

Maybe she was just going to get her period? She wasn't normally affected by PMS, but…maybe. Besides, she was probably due for her period. She did some quick mental calculations, but couldn't remember how long it had been.

"Hello?"

Shit. Jess was early. Cynthia grabbed a tampon to shove in her purse, just in case.

"Hey, Jess." She left the bathroom and headed into the small kitchen, where Jess had already started to prepare her mother's tea and morning meds. The woman had really been a godsend and Cynthia had to resist the urge to hug her. Jess had been working for her since the beginning of the New Year, but even in only two months, Cynthia was coming to see Jess as part of her little family. She was so good with her mother and being almost the same age as herself, it was kind of nice to have her around. Almost like a sister. Or at least a friend, and she could do with a few more of those these days.

"How was she last night?" Jess moved around the kitchen with an easy familiarity and prepared the tray. "Did she sleep through?"

Cynthia nodded. "I think so. If she woke up, I didn't hear her." She accepted the mug of coffee that Jess handed her, but instantly her nose revolted at the smell and she put it on the counter behind her, opting for a cup of tea instead.

"You're still off coffee, hey?" Jess noticed Cynthia's reaction. "What's up with that?"

"I have no idea. And I really could use it, too. I'm so tired these days."

Jess handed her the cream before she turned to grab the toast that had just popped. "You've been working too hard. Your mom said you've been coming in really late."

Cynthia didn't bother to tell Jess the real reason she'd been coming home late. For the last week, every day after she closed up the shop, she'd made a point to go up to the ski hill and visit Nala and her pups. It was cold and the temperature could drop quickly in the mountains, so Cynthia made sure the dogs had fresh blankets and Nala had fresh food and of course some love and attention. She also didn't bother mentioning that more than once, she'd run into Seth in the maintenance shed and they'd spent some time talking until she couldn't actually remember if it was the dogs or the man she'd gone to see in the first place.

No, there was no point telling Jess any of that. Especially if she might share the information with her mother. The very last thing she needed was her mom to start worrying about her love life, as messed up as it was. Her mother had enough to focus on. It was best she kept her relationship with Seth a secret for now. Especially because it was more like a non-relationship. Nothing had happened between them.

Except for that kiss on Valentine's Day.

She felt her cheeks flush at the memory of his lips on hers.

"Are you okay, Cynthia?" Jess stared at her. "You're not coming down with something, are you? Because if you are, you should probably stay away from your—"

"I'm fine." Cynthia forced herself to smile. "In fact, I'll take Mom her breakfast before I head out."

"If you're sure." It was clear by the way she looked at her that Jess didn't believe that everything was fine, but Cynthia didn't care. She wouldn't put her mom at risk if she wasn't feeling—

Her stomach rolled, and she dropped the tray back to the counter before she ran to the bathroom and emptied the contents of her mostly empty stomach into the toilet.

She couldn't be sick. She didn't feel sick and she didn't know anyone who'd had the flu recently. It was probably just something she ate. Cynthia got up, rinsed her mouth and was about to head back into the kitchen when Jess appeared in the doorway.

"Are you..."

Cynthia nodded. "I'm totally fine. Honestly, it must have been something I ate."

Jess frowned and shook her head. "You know...when my

sister was pregnant, she couldn't stand the smell of coffee either. And her morning sickness would come on without—"

"I'm not pregnant." She shook her head and glared at Jess. "It's not even a possibility."

"Okay, well, you'd know, right?" Jess giggled uncertainly. "I just thought, all your symptoms, they're kind of—"

"I'm not," Cynthia said again.

The other woman nodded and Cynthia wiped her mouth before she stood slowly. "I forgot about your sister," she said. Jess's sister was a few years older than Cynthia, and they'd never been friends, but it was big news in town when Zoe Alderman had found herself knocked up in the tenth grade. Her parents had shipped her off somewhere to have the baby and when she'd returned to town, she was no longer the party girl she had been. It was as if the light had been dimmed inside her. Right after graduation, she moved away and had never been back as far as Cynthia knew.

"Yeah." Jess nodded. "It was a long time ago. But even when you're little, things like that are hard to forget."

A silence grew between them and Cynthia bit her bottom lip before she said again, "Well, I'm not pregnant. There's no way. I must just have a bit of a bug or something."

"Right. Well, then I guess I better take breakfast into Linda. Just in case."

"Yes." Cynthia nodded, only half listening. "That's probably best."

Jess looked as though she might say something else, but to Cynthia's relief she only bit her lip before she left her alone in the bathroom. Her words raced through Cynthia's head. *Pregnant.* All at once the room was too warm. She backed up until her back was pressed against the wall and she slipped to the floor. Her mind tried to do some quick calculations. There was New Year's Eve. But she'd had her cycle after that, hadn't she? Maybe she hadn't. But...

And then there was that one other time.

She'd tried so hard to convince herself it hadn't happened. That she wasn't *that* girl. The type who hooked up with a guy, not once but twice. She *wasn't* that girl. It was a momentary blip of insanity. Everyone was allowed to make mistakes and Cynthia had managed to convince herself that her slip in her moral standards had been due to all the stress she'd been under. That same stress that was obviously affecting her menstrual cycle.

She desperately tried to work out the math in her head and as soon as she had, Cynthia almost threw up again. She was late. Really late. How had she not noticed? Sure, her period wasn't always like clockwork like some women, but it was never...no. Certainly she'd get her period any day now. She'd been busy and under a lot of stress, that was all.

But even as Cynthia finally pulled herself off the bathroom floor and headed out the door to open the shop, the only thing she'd convinced herself of was that she needed to take a pregnancy test. As soon as possible.

THE SUN HAD JUST STARTED to dip below the mountains when Seth finally finished locking up the mid-mountain lodge that served as a place for skiers to warm up and grab a cup of coffee or bowl of soup when they were ready to take a break from the slopes. It had been his idea to open the smaller lodge to keep people on the hill instead of having to ski to the base to get something to eat. And it had been a good idea, too. By keeping people out on the hill, it had really alleviated long lineups at the base chairlifts, which made for happier skiers, which made for a happier bottom line when they kept coming back.

In reality, he probably didn't have to lock up at all. Once

the hill was closed, there wouldn't be anyone so far out who would break in. But then again, he was a teenager once and had certainly gotten in his fair share of trouble. It was better to be safe. He tucked his keys into his pocket and clicked his boots into his skis. Some days he opted to take a snowmobile up to do his rounds, but the snow had been falling steadily all day, and when there was fresh powder to enjoy, there was no decision to make. It was all about the skiing.

A few stragglers were still on the back runs, but for the most part, Seth had the hill to himself. And he took full advantage of it. Normally, he'd head for the trees, and the deeper, likely untouched snow in there, but late in the afternoon with the light so flat, it was better to stay on the open runs. He hit the hard bump of snow, planted his pole and pushed hard around another one, moving into the next one hard and fast, taking it like a pro. Seth thrived on the moguls, letting his knees come together in a hard bounce one after another until finally he came to a skidding stop, snow flying in an arcing fan as he finished the run.

It felt good. Damn good and it was the best way he knew to work out frustration. Especially frustration of a sexual nature. There was another way he knew of, but the only one he wanted to work out with seemed to be Cynthia. Much to his annoyance. He'd tried to hit on a gorgeous woman in the ski lodge earlier, but his heart wasn't into it, and he ended up buying her a cup of coffee and wishing her a good day.

But he had to get Cynthia out of his head. Enough was enough. If she wasn't interested in him, he'd move on. And that's exactly what he planned to do. Just as soon as he was finished up at the hill, his plan was to head down to the Grizzly Paw, have a few beers and find himself some hot young thing to take his mind off a certain redhead. He'd checked in on Nala and her pups earlier so he wouldn't chance running into her.

Cynthia had been visiting the dogs in the evening like clockwork, and up until now he'd looked forward to the visits, even planning his own schedule around seeing her. But not tonight. No way. If he saw her, if he laid eyes on that body that never failed to make his cock twitch, he knew exactly what he'd do and it wouldn't involve finding anyone new to warm his bed. Even though that was exactly what he needed.

He waved at a few of the lifties who were closing down the chairlift for the day. Normally he'd go chat with them, but with the sun going down, and the mass of people all heading for their cars, he knew he was running out of time before Cynthia would show up. He clicked his poles into his bindings and popped out of his skis, picking them up and tossing them over his shoulder with ease before determinedly heading away from the maintenance shed and into his office to finish up for the day.

IT TOOK him longer than he would have liked to get his work wrapped up and it was already past dinnertime by the time Seth headed down the mountain and into town. After a quick stop at home for a shower and change, Seth was on his way to the Grizzly Paw. And for the first time in a long time, he looked forward to a night out that, if he had any luck at all, would end up with some company in his bed. He needed to get Cynthia out of his head and prove to himself that he wasn't fixated on a woman who wanted nothing to do with him. That had never been his style and he wasn't about to start now.

It was a Friday night in the middle of ski season, and the Paw was already pretty busy by the time Seth walked through the door at quarter to eight. Not only was the Paw the best place to kick off the weekend with good friends, it was the only bar in town, which made it an easy choice for a Friday night. Even if there had been options, Seth knew he'd still choose the

Paw. When he walked through the big wooden doors, he felt at home.

The bar was everything a rustic, small-town bar should be: large slab wood tables and a cozy, rustic feel. Seth squeezed his way through the growing crowd and headed straight up to the bar where Archer Wolfe greeted him with a smile and a wave.

"Hey, man." Seth sank into an empty barstool so he could survey his surroundings before he committed to anything. "Busy in here tonight."

"It is." Archer slid a frothy pint across the glossy wooden bar. "Business has been good lately. Sam's pretty happy about it. Except when she has to wait tables." He pointed across the room where Samantha Harrison, the owner of the Grizzly Paw, was delivering a round of drinks to a table of women he didn't recognize.

Seth laughed at the sight because they all knew that Sam hated waiting tables unless she was serving a group of her friends and then sitting down to join them. He also made note of the women. He'd have to check them out a little later. He turned back to Archer and took a long pull on his drink. "I guess she hasn't found anyone to replace Kylie yet?"

Archer shook his head. "Not yet. But she hasn't been looking very hard. If you ask me, I think she was secretly hoping Kylie would decide nursing school wasn't for her and ask for her job back."

"Like that would happen."

"Exactly." Archer smiled. "But it's keeping her busy at least. And she's certainly not going to complain about being busy." He shook his head and used a bar towel to wipe an already clean spot on the bar. "So what's new with you? Things good up the hill? I haven't seen you around lately."

Seth took another long drink and wiped his mouth with the back of his hand before he answered. "It's been good. The snow's great, lots of people, and from what I hear, more to come. We're working on some big plans for a spring ski Slush Cup in April before we shut down. Should be fun."

"Should be," Archer agreed. "Maybe we can see about coming up to serve some beer and chili or something. I'll talk to Sam."

The two men chatted for a few more minutes, falling into the easy chatter of longtime friends, and Seth relaxed into the atmosphere of the Paw. When Archer nodded at a customer farther down the bar before he excused himself to serve her, Seth used the opportunity to look around a bit more. He noticed the group of women he'd spotted earlier—they were good-looking and a few of them didn't have wedding rings on —but they were putting out a *girls' night* vibe and Seth knew enough than to get in the middle of that type of situation.

Rhys Anderson and his girlfriend Kari sat at a table tucked in the corner and looked to be having some sort of romantic date night. He'd stop by to say hi, but not yet. Seth finished his beer, and continued to scan the room. He recognized Jax Carver and Bria Sheridan. He didn't know them very well, but he did know that Cynthia dated Jax briefly before he settled down with Bria. An irrational heat of jealousy flared inside him and he looked away.

It was ridiculous. He wasn't supposed to be thinking about Cynthia. That was the whole point of the night. To not think about Cynthia.

He did one more sweep of the room with his eyes before finally he returned his gaze to the table of women, who were now doing shots. One of the women, a blond with a low cut t-shirt and a smoldering stare that pinned him from across the room, lifted her glass, looked right at him and winked before she downed the drink.

He knew what would come next. He'd smile at her and tip his head in invite. In a few minutes, the woman would excuse herself and make her way over to the bar, where she'd lean up against him and make sure he could see down her top. She'd casually suggest that Seth by her a drink; he would, and then another. Soon they'd find their way into the empty space in the middle of the bar that acted as a dance floor on nights like this, he'd kiss her, and then he'd take her home.

Seth pressed his lips together and turned around on his stool, closing down the offer before it became one.

"She seems like a nice girl."

Startled, he looked up to see Samantha behind the bar as she filled her tray with glasses.

"Hey, Sam." He smiled and then shook his head. "Who seems nice?"

She gave him a look that told him she wasn't buying his Mr. Innocent act. "The blond. She's in town with some friends for a stagette. They're headed up to the Springs tomorrow for some spa treatments, but tonight it's all about a good time." Sam made little curls with her fingers. "And I quote."

Seth laughed and without asking, Sam poured him another beer. "So what makes you think I'd be interested in her?"

She handed him the beer. "Seriously? Who isn't your type?"

He tipped his head, but didn't bother to disagree. "I'm not interested tonight." He'd only said that to get Sam off his back, but the second the words passed his lips, he realized it was true. He wasn't interested.

"Well, you may have to rethink that," Sam said with a sly smile and gestured behind him before she picked up the full tray and disappeared into the crowd.

He knew without turning around what he'd see, and sure enough, seconds later the scent of heavy perfume filled the air around him. He took one more sip of his beer and turned so he stared directly at the very well-endowed chest of the blond woman. His body clearly had a different idea than his mind, if the twitch in his crotch was any indication. Seth took his time trailing his eyes up the woman's body until their eyes met.

"I'm Holly." She didn't offer her hand but instead put a hand on her hip and thrust her chest forward.

He nodded in approval as instinct and old habits took over. "Well, Holly. It looks like your drink is empty. Let's see what we can do about that."

CYNTHIA DIDN'T THINK Suzy Crosswell was ever going to leave. Technically, the Store Room closed at nine on Friday nights, but when Suzy ran in the door at ten to, she couldn't say no. Especially considering the other woman ran the bakery, Dream Puffs, and regularly supplied Cynthia with a muffin and a latte for breakfast. She wasn't going to turn away her baked goods connection.

Normally she'd have Colton close up but there was some sort of dance at the high school and he'd been desperate for the night off so he could take a date. Who was she to stand in the way of young love? So, like the softie she was, she'd given him the night off, which meant Cynthia had to endure Suzy's inquiries on her mom's health and how she was doing.

She knew her mom and Suzy had once been good friends. As single women running businesses in Cedar Springs, they'd stuck together in the early days. Cynthia wasn't sure what had happened to pull them apart or if they'd just drifted apart as their lives got busy. Her mother didn't really talk about it and besides Suzy asking after Linda and occasionally dropping off baked goods for her, she never offered to visit for herself, and for some reason, Cynthia never brought it up.

When Suzy was finally done paying for her things and Cynthia locked the door behind her and flicked off the "open" sign, she suddenly wished the other woman would come back.

Not because she enjoyed her company that much, but because it would act as a distraction for what she needed to do next.

Her eyes moved to the aisle where she stocked the feminine products: tampons, pads, and pregnancy tests. She'd managed to find excuses all day as to why she should wait, but she couldn't put it off too much longer. Especially because the longer she went without actually taking the test, the more she knew in her heart what the result would be. She may not have had time to take the test, but she had found time to do the mental calculations that told her exactly what she didn't want to hear.

There was no point putting it off any longer. Before she could find another reason not to, Cynthia marched herself up the aisle and without spending any time on the selection, grabbed three different boxes, shoved them in her tote bag and flicked off the lights before she locked the door to the shop behind her.

Once she was outside, she paused, took a deep breath and filled her lungs with the crisp wintery air.

What now?

She could go home and take the test. No, she *should* go home and take the test. But she couldn't face it. Not yet. Normally, she'd get in her car and head up to the ski hill to see the puppies the way she'd been doing every night. But what if Seth was there?

It had been kind of nice running into Seth up at the hill, but there was no way she could make small talk with him and discuss puppy names as if there wasn't three different pregnancy tests sitting in her bag ready to determine the rest of her life.

And his.

The thought scared the hell out of her, and she refused to entertain it even for a second.

She needed a distraction. A burst of music caught her

attention and Cynthia's gaze drifted down the street to where the Grizzly Paw sat at the end, right before the beach and the still frozen lake. On a Friday night, the Paw would be packed and she was sure to find some of her friends inside. It would be good to lose herself in the daily gossip and news of her friends. Especially if it meant putting off her own gossip for a few more hours.

She tugged her tote bag higher up on her arm and headed down the street. Even if the pub was full of tourists and skiers, at the very least Samantha would be there and with Kylie back in Vancouver getting set up for her classes for the next few days, Sam was the closest thing she had to a best friend at the moment.

Just as she knew it would be, the Grizzly Paw was packed. Business had been good for all the businesses in town since Trent and Dylan Harrison opened the Springs up the hill, and now with Stone Summit, their sleepy little town had been totally transformed. Not that Cynthia was complaining. Not at all; the new business made it possible for her store to stay open and if it wasn't for all the other bills she had to deal with, she might actually be seeing a profit.

But despite all the good the tourists brought with them, there were times when Cynthia couldn't help but wish for the good old days when she could walk into the Paw and not have to dodge around a bunch of strangers in order to find her friends. She did her best to scan the room through the thick of bodies. Her eyes landed first on Jax and Bria. The other woman caught her eye, so Cynthia nodded and gave her a friendly smile, but continued to look.

It's not that they didn't like each other, but Bria Sheridan had been a tricky woman to get to know ever since she moved to town. And to be fair, Cynthia hadn't put much of an effort in either. Mostly because it had been her fault that Bria and Jax had almost split up when Cynthia made the very bad decision to sell private pictures of musician Slade Black's proposal to local single mom, Beth Martin. It had been a mistake. A very bad mistake and it had cost her a few friendships, and definitely more than enough hurt for all those involved, but Cynthia had been desperate. It was right after her mother's diagnosis had come in and she needed the extra money to pay for a new experimental drug. Not that it worked. And she knew the ends didn't justify the means, but the whole situation was in the past. At least for most people.

She kept looking around the room and was surprised that she didn't see more people she recognized. She'd almost convinced herself to just turn around and head home when her eyes landed on Sam up at the bar, pulling beer at the tap. Sam looked up and waved at her with a bright smile. It was nice to see a friendly face. With her bag close to her side, she pushed her way through the crowd and maneuvered her way up to the bar. Sam put down the beer, wiped her hands and pulled Cynthia into a hug.

"How've you been?" Sam asked when she released her. "I haven't seen you in forever. Everything okay? How's your mom?"

"So many questions." Cynthia laughed. "Mom's good. I've been around, just busy. But who isn't these days?" She gestured with one hand. "Speaking of busy. Wow."

"I know, right? And ever since Kylie quit...well, let's just say I better hire someone quick before I lose my mind." She continued to talk, but went back behind the bar. "Are you going to stay awhile? I'll grab you a drink."

"I was kind of hoping to run into someone, but it looks like the place is packed with visitors tonight." She didn't bother mentioning that she'd already seen Jax and Bria; Sam would know better than to think Cynthia would sit down with them. At least not without a group of others.

"Rhys and Kari are here," Sam said. "They're just

finishing dinner." She pointed and Cynthia looked across the room, but instead of seeing the couple, her eyes landed on Seth McBride at the other end of the bar. Sam must have noticed where Cynthia looked because she added, "Seth's here, too. But...well, you know Seth."

Cynthia nodded, unable to take her eyes off his strong back. "I do."

Sam looked at her strangely for a second. "Hey, I have to deliver these drinks, but if you hang out for a minute, I'll grab you a drink and we can chat. At least until between rounds out there."

She nodded and watched Sam disappear with the full tray of drinks. She might as well stay for a few minutes. Maybe she'd pop over and say hi to Rhys and Kari, too. She'd gone to school with Rhys, and really liked his girlfriend, who was fairly new to town. She fit right into the group and despite being a little shy at first, was an absolute sweetheart.

Going to talk to her friends would have been the right thing to do, but she didn't move. Instead, she watched Seth for a moment. He sat alone, sipping a beer and looking way too damn good. What was he doing alone? Seth McBride was never alone on a Friday night. But that was before...well, before them. Come to think of it, she hadn't seen him with another woman in weeks.

Even if her brain didn't want to acknowledge the reaction he had on her, her body wasn't getting the same message. A heat grew between her legs just by looking at him.

It was so wrong for her to have any feelings for him at all. He was all wrong. But he'd been different lately and the way he looked after the puppies...he was sweet and tender, just the way a daddy should be.

No.

She shook her head, hard.

There was no way she'd let herself think like that. Not yet.

Not ever. Her purse grew heavier on her arm, as if the three boxes tucked inside took on the weight of what they could reveal. It didn't matter what the test results were: he was still Seth McBride.

As if he knew she was thinking about him, Seth slowly turned around in his seat and when he saw her watching him, his face split into a wide smile. Her stomach flipped and her nipples peaked under the sweater she wore. His effect on her was instant and undeniable. She knew she shouldn't but she couldn't help it. Cynthia returned his smile.

He raised one eyebrow. In invitation? He was sitting alone and they had been enjoying each other's company lately.

Why not?

She had a million reasons not to, and one potentially huge reason not to, but Cynthia was so tired of thinking. She just needed to act. Even if acting meant simply spending a little time talking to man. Why couldn't it be that simple? At least for one night.

Without overanalyzing it more than she already had, Cynthia squeezed her way through the crowd, making her way to the other end of the bar where Seth sat. There were more people than she thought, and she bobbed and weaved through them until he was right there in front of her.

With a blond.

Where had she come from? The woman put her purse down on the bar and slipped an arm around Seth's neck, using her other hand to ruffle through his hair while she leaned in and whispered something in his ear.

Cynthia froze. The noise around her all but disappeared as she stared at the scene in front of her. Seth's mouth curled up into his sexy smile at whatever it was she was saying to him. Something dirty, no doubt.

Had she been there all along?

Was he on a date?

No. He'd likely just picked her up that night. That's how Seth worked. It's how he always worked. She'd been stupid to think even for a second that he'd changed.

Her stomach rolled and the room tilted as reality crashed into her. Seth wasn't different. He was the same old womanizing SOB who was also the father of the child she knew without a doubt she was carrying. She didn't need a test to prove what she already knew deep down to be the truth. Her hand flew to her stomach and a sound, somewhere between a hysterical laugh and a sob, rose from her throat.

She had to get out of there.

Suddenly, all the people who were only a moment ago crushing her with their proximity were gone, leaving her exposed and directly in Seth's line of vision.

"Cynthia."

No. She couldn't talk to him.

"Cyn? Wait."

She spun around wildly; she needed to get away. Fast. Her tote bag caught on something and as she moved forward, her bag was wrenched from her arm.

"No!" She turned and futilely tried to grab at the bag, but it was too late.

Her tote crashed to the floor. The contents scattered.

Numb, she stared at the items for a fraction of a second before she knelt on the hardwood and randomly grabbed for her things.

"Cynthia. Stop." Seth was there. She didn't look up to confirm it, but she could feel him. "Here," he said. "Let me help."

She shook her head. "No. I got it." She needed to get the boxes before he saw them. Her hands blindly scrabbled for her wallet, her keys, one box, another and then—

"What's this?"

She looked up and finally met his eyes.

"Cynthia?"

She didn't have to look at what he held in his hand to know what it was.

"Is this…"

To keep from shattering into a million pieces right there in front of everyone, Cynthia's gaze didn't waver as she reached out, took the pregnancy test from his hand and shoved it into her bag.

Chapter Four

"CYNTHIA! WAIT!"

She didn't even turn around as she pushed her way through the crowd and out the front door of the Paw. Seth's brain spun with the scene that had just played out.

What the hell had just happened?

From somewhere behind him, he could hear Holly calling his name but he ignored her just the way he should have when she'd approached him at the bar. Dammit. He knew he should have gone with his gut and just left well enough alone. He didn't want some half-drunk blond out for a good time. He wanted—hell. He didn't know what he wanted.

But at least for the moment, the only thing he wanted was to find Cynthia and find out why the hell she had a pregnancy test in her purse.

He didn't bother grabbing his jacket or clearing up his bill. There was no time. He needed to get to Cynthia. Now.

Seth shoved his way through the crowd and into the cold March night. Spring usually came late in the mountains, and by the chill in the air, it certainly wouldn't be coming that night.

"Cynthia!"

He looked up the street toward the Store Room. She wasn't there. He turned toward the lake. There. On the beach was the shadowy shape of a woman, her arms wrapped around her body, her hair flying in the breeze. Cynthia.

He jogged over to her, and grabbed her arm to force her to turn around. When he saw the look on her face, he regretted the forceful approach. Shit. He wasn't handling things very well.

"Sorry." He let go of her and dropped his hands. "What you saw…that woman…it's not…"

She shook her head and turned away. "It doesn't matter."

"It does."

It did. He didn't know why exactly, but it mattered. A lot.

"It's really none of my business what or who you do, Seth. We're not…well, we're not anything." She shrugged but he wasn't dumb enough to think she was brushing it off. He also wasn't stupid enough to think he'd be able to convince her differently. At least not at the moment.

"Cynthia." He took her hands in his and gently turned her so she faced him. She looked down at their feet, but she didn't pull away from his hands. He kept his voice low. "What's in the box?"

She was quiet and for a moment he wondered whether she'd heard him. But then she said, "It's nothing."

"It looked like something." She shook her head but he wasn't going to let her run again. "Why do you have a pregnancy test?"

Speaking the words aloud caused a tightening in his gut. Cynthia wasn't like him. She didn't sleep around; she didn't have flings and meaningless relationships. If she had a pregnancy test in her purse…no. They used protection. They'd been safe. There had to be another explanation. And surely there would be.

She'd tell him it was from the store and she'd forgotten to put it away. Or that it was for a friend. *Kylie.* Maybe Kylie and Malcolm were pregnant?

Even as the options ran through his head, he knew they were all bullshit and after what felt like forever, when Cynthia finally looked up and looked into his eyes, he knew it for a fact. Even in the dim evening light, with only the moon and the distant streetlights to illuminate them, he could see the spark in their deep green depths. She spoke slowly and with an edge he'd never heard from her before. "It's really none of your concern."

He knew then that it most definitely was his concern. For all her bravado, she was a terrible liar. Seth's gut twisted, hard. "Cynthia, I—"

"I told you." She tried to turn away from him again. "It's none of your business."

"Bullshit."

She snapped her head around. Her eyes flared with anger; a hot blush he could see even in the night light heated her face. "Pardon me?"

"It is my concern and I think we both know it."

She stared at him, and Seth was positive she was going to deny it again, or pull away or even smack him across the face. Instead, her face fell and she dropped her head.

His heart broke a little bit to see her cry and know that he might very well be responsible for those tears. He released her hands and instead put two fingers under her chin and tilted it up so he could see her tear-streaked face. "Don't cry. It's going to be okay." A thought occurred to him. "You still have the box, right?"

She nodded. "Three."

"Three?"

She made a sound that was half a sob and half a laugh. "I have three boxes."

"Three boxes?" Seth was aware he sounded like a broken record, but his brain was having more than a little bit of trouble trying to process what she was talking about.

Cynthia reached into her pocket, pulled out a tissue and wiped her nose. "I've never done this before, and I...I didn't know what to get so I just thought it might be...it doesn't matter."

"Okay." He nodded in an effort to look calmer than he was feeling, which was about as far from calm as he had ever been. "First things first. You have to take the test."

Panic crossed Cynthia's face for a moment before she nodded. "I do. But..."

"Come on. Let's go." He took her hand and started to walk, but she didn't move and he jerked back. "Cynthia?"

She shook her head. "I can't."

"You have to."

"No. I mean...I can't do it at my house. My mom...I—"

"We'll go to my place." He started to walk again, the matter settled. Once more, he jerked backward when she didn't walk along with him. Seth turned and raised his eyebrow in question.

"No." She shook her head. "This isn't your—"

"So help me." With one step, he closed the distance between them. "If you say one more time that this isn't my problem, I will—" He broke off, not quite knowing how to finish his threat, but it didn't matter because by the flush in her cheeks and the heaving of her chest, Seth knew he'd gotten his point across. Clearly. "I'm taking you back to my place, and you're going to take that test. And that's the end of it."

She opened her mouth, no doubt to protest again, but he'd heard all the protests he could handle for one night. He wrapped one large hand behind her head, pulled her in to meet his lips and kissed her hard. When he was done, he looked into her beautiful green eyes. "Let's go. It's freezing out here."

THERE WAS no way she was going back into the Paw, and even though Seth didn't believe her when she said she would wait outside for him while he went to get his jacket that had his truck keys, she wasn't going anywhere. He'd eyed her suspiciously and looked over his shoulder at least twice before he disappeared inside. The truth was, she wasn't going anywhere. She just didn't have the energy.

She had to take the test and although the last place she thought she'd be doing it was at Seth's house, she no longer cared.

He reappeared only moments later, tugging his leather jacket over his shoulders; Cynthia's stomach fluttered at the way his t-shirt pulled up and exposed a sliver of stomach. That, combined with the kiss he'd given her on the beach, caused all kinds of thoughts to flash through her head. Thoughts that she shut down before they could become ideas.

Damn, that's what got her into this situation in the first place.

"Ready?" He opened the door to his truck without waiting for a response and she climbed into the cab, careful not to drop her tote bag.

They didn't speak on the short drive to Seth's place. She waited quietly as he unlocked the door and went around the space, turning on lights. She'd been there before, of course, but she'd never paid much attention to her surroundings. It was definitely the home of a single man: sparsely decorated, but clean. Cynthia stood awkwardly in the living room, unsure what to do next. Should she just go straight to the bathroom, pee on the stick and determine the rest of their lives? Or maybe they'd make small talk first?

"Do you need something to drink?"

Small talk it was. Cynthia released the breath she'd been holding.

"You know, so you can…"

The smile fell off her face as she caught up to what he was thinking.

"I'm good, thanks. I'll just go to the bathroom."

"It's down the hall."

She looked over her shoulder and smiled weakly. "I remember."

And she did remember. She remembered waking up and sneaking out of Seth's bed on New Year's Day. She'd stood in the very spot she stood now and looked in the mirror at her reflection. At the time, she remembered being surprised at herself that she would go home with Seth. She wasn't the type of woman who did one-night stands. She didn't regret it, though. How could she? It was the best sex she'd ever had. And as it turned out, it wasn't a one-night stand. Two weeks later, they'd done it again. That time she had regretted it. Cynthia had stood in that very same bathroom, staring in that very same mirror, and wanted to cry because the second time with Seth had been different.

The second time they'd hooked up, it was more than just sex, at least to her. She didn't want to, but dammit, she'd felt something between them. Something she wanted to keep feeling.

Cynthia took a deep breath and nodded at her reflection.

Time to get it over with.

Cynthia rummaged through her bag and pulled out the three boxes and lined them up on the counter. Now the question was, which test should she take? She picked up the first box and read the back.

If two purple bands appear, the result is positive.

What does positive mean? Cynthia stared at the stick and blinked hard. *Positive in the sense that I'm not pregnant? Because that would be a positive.*

She put the box down and picked up the next one.

A positive result is indicated by a blue happy face.

Again, that word. That's assuming the person taking the test agrees that that's a positive situation. Particularly with the addition of the happy face.

A knock on the door jolted her. "Are you okay in there? Can I do anything?"

She would have laughed if she wasn't so freaked out. Instead, she opened the door and let him in.

"I don't know which one to take."

Seth scanned the boxes on his bathroom counter, his eyebrows knitted together. "Hmm. What's the difference?"

"Purple bands, happy faces, positives that aren't positive at all and—"

He put his hand on her shoulder. "Take a breath."

She looked at his face and instantly settled. He had to be freaking out as much as she was, but if he was, he didn't show it. Seth was the epitome of calm and collected. She did as he said.

"Good."

He smiled and she felt better. Never in a million years did she think that she'd be in this situation, especially with Seth. But at that moment, she was glad that if it had to be with anyone, it was with him.

"Feel better?"

She nodded and shrugged at the same time.

"Good, I think." He let go of her arm and picked up the boxes. "Let me worry about this. Why don't you just pee on all of them and I'll read the instructions and figure out how to decipher it? Does that work?"

Cynthia nodded again because it sounded like the best plan she'd heard.

Seth quickly opened the packages and handed her three sticks. "I'll just be out there, okay?"

She nodded again, like a bobblehead doll, and waited until Seth closed the door behind him before she got down to business. Might as well just get it over with. Besides, it felt infinitely better to only be in charge of one part of the testing process.

As soon as she was done, she washed up and left the sticks lined up on the bathroom counter before she went out to join Seth in the living room. He had all the boxes lined up with the instructions spread open all over the coffee table. He stood when he saw her and held out his hand, but she shook her head and sat in the chair across from him.

"I guess we wait now," he said. "They all say to wait between about two and five minutes."

"Okay." She was going to nod again, but stopped herself. "Thank you."

"I'm just glad I could be here to help. I mean, it's not like this is all on you, right? I'm just as responsible." His face shifted and he scowled. "I mean...I am, right? It's my—"

"Yes." She shot him a look and jumped up from her chair, unable to sit any longer. "I don't make it a habit to sleep around, Seth. Not like..." She stopped herself before she said anything more.

"Of course." He ran his hand through his hair. "I'm sorry. I know you don't. I just thought...I mean, we used a condom and everything."

"I know, but they're only like ninety-eight percent effective." Cynthia couldn't stop herself from bursting out into a maniacal laugh. "Someone's got to be in that two percent, right? Why wouldn't it be me?"

Seth moved quickly and stood in front of her, his face serious. "Us, remember?"

Two simple words and Cynthia thought she'd cry again. She swallowed hard and forced the tears back. "We're getting a little ahead of ourselves here. I mean, we don't even...we should wait and see what it says." Even as she spoke the words, she knew in her heart what all three of the sticks would say.

"No matter what the tests say, Cynthia." He reached up and touched her cheek with so much tenderness, Cynthia had to force herself to focus on what he was saying. "I really like spending time with you and...hell, I'm not good with words." His hand slipped around and cupped the back of her head, pulling her into his kiss for the second time that night.

For a moment, Cynthia let herself forget why they were there and lost herself in the taste of him, but as much as she wanted to let herself totally go, she couldn't. The reason they were there, standing in his living room in the first place, hung over them like a heavy cloud. She pulled back.

"It's probably time." She reached up and touched her lips; she wanted to savor the moment, no matter how small, before her life changed forever.

Chapter Five

SETH STARED at Cynthia for a moment before he realized what she'd said. Of course it was time. He glanced at his watch. Five minutes had passed. It was past time. Although he could easily stand there and kiss her all night. And given the choice of activities, there would be no contest.

But they couldn't put it off forever.

"Do you need the—" Cynthia gestured to the instruction sheets he'd memorized.

"Nope. I think it's pretty straightforward. Two purple bars, a smiley face," he shook his head at that one, "and the word *pregnant*. I don't think we can mess that up."

She nodded and repeated, "Two purple bars. A happy face. Pregnant. Got it."

Together they walked down the hall to the bathroom door. He waited for her to open it. Somehow it seemed right that she be the one to check the tests. But Cynthia didn't move. He took her hand and squeezed. "It's going to be okay, Cyn. No matter what the tests say. I meant what I said a minute ago."

She dropped her head for a second before she looked up at

him. He couldn't read the expression on her face. It wasn't sad, or scared—more like…resigned. "You look," she said simply.

"Cynthia, I think—"

"I already know what they say."

Seth stared at her for a second longer before he willed his body to move forward. He walked into the bathroom and looked down at the counter.

Two purple bars. A happy face. Pregnant.

In a rush, all the blood drained from his face. He looked again.

Two purple bars. A happy face. Pregnant.

He swallowed hard and forced himself to stay calm. Cynthia would need him to be calm. She'd need him to be strong and steady and a voice of reason. She was a strong woman, sure. But this…this. Damn. Cynthia had enough on her plate and—*Cynthia.*

He spun around to tell her what the result was but she was gone.

"Cynthia?"

Seth sprinted down the hall, half expecting her to have run again. But she hadn't. She sat on the couch, staring straight ahead, and when she saw him, she gave him a weak smile. "Congratulations."

She'd known.

It was the first thought when he saw her face and heard the word come out of her mouth. She'd known the whole time what the tests would say.

"You knew?"

She shrugged. "Not until I saw your face. But I guess from the moment I thought it might be a possibility, I've known."

"How long has that been?"

She laughed. "Only since this morning."

"That's it? Really?" He moved to the couch and sat next to

her. "Don't women keep track of these things and mark it on a calendar or something?"

"I've been a little preoccupied. Besides, does it matter?"

"No."

"I guess we should figure out what we're going to do."

He shook his head. "Not tonight."

"Why not—"

"Because tonight, I need you to know something," he said. "And really know it. Not just think that you know it, but I want you to feel it deep in your bones."

"What?"

He slid one hand onto her thigh, and reached for her with the other. He pulled her close. "What I said earlier…I meant it." When she tried to object, he put his finger on her lips to silence her. "I like spending time with you, Cynthia."

"Well, that's a good thing," she quipped. "Because it looks like we're going to—"

"Seriously, woman," he growled and before she could say another word, he kissed her hard. All the pent-up emotion of the last few hours flowed out of him. He knew there were a million other things he should be doing. Or saying. Hell, they probably should be talking about their options, about what the hell they were going to do now. They should be talking about how they felt, and he knew he was being an asshole. The gentlemanly thing to do would be to hold her, let her cry and ask her how she was feeling.

But he was far from a gentleman, at least at that moment. And there'd be time for talking later. For now, he needed to be close to her, he needed to feel her, and maybe he'd be able to express everything he was feeling without any words at all.

He felt the exact moment she realized what he was trying to do with his avoidance strategy, and to his relief, instead of pushing him away or forcing him to have a conversation he was not remotely ready to have, Cynthia opened her mouth to him and kissed him in return.

It didn't make any sense to consummate the news they just got with the very act that got them there in the first place, but that wasn't what Seth was thinking about as he slid Cynthia's sweater up and over her head. All he could focus on was the amazing woman beneath him and the undeniable chemistry they had. Everything else could wait. He trailed kisses down her neck, nibbling the sensitive spot behind her ear the way she liked, before he moved his kisses farther south.

Seth took a moment to gaze at the swell of her breasts that were all but bursting out of her pink lacy bra. They were different. Bigger, fuller. Not that he didn't like everything about her breasts before—because he definitely did—but his mouth watered at the sight of Cynthia's new voluptuous curves.

She must have sensed his hesitation. "They're a bit…well, I know they're…I just thought I was gaining weight."

He looked up to see the blush in her face that quickly crept down to her chest. There was nothing he liked more than the flush of her skin, but under no circumstances did he want it if there was any insecurity behind it. Especially because the woman had nothing to be insecure about. At all.

"You're gorgeous."

"I'm different," she protested. "I'm—"

"Perfect." He gently ran his thumbs over her nipples, and they responded instantly, straining through the lace just the way he knew they would. "You are absolutely perfect." He didn't wait for a response before he lowered his mouth to first one breast and suckled her hard tip through her bra. She arched her back and groaned in response. He looked up quickly and gave her a wicked grin before he turned his attention to the other breast. She responded again with a low groan from deep in her throat.

His erection strained at the fly of his jeans and Seth knew

if he slid his hands into her panties, she'd be completely wet for him already. In fact, that was a damn good idea. Wrapping his arms around her, he shifted Cynthia on the couch, so she laid down the length of the sofa. He sat back and undid the buckle of her jeans before he slipped the denim over her hips and down her legs. Her matching pink panties that were little more than a scrap between her legs almost made him explode on the spot.

"Perfect," he said again.

He stripped his shirt off over his head, and quickly shed his jeans before he turned his attentions back to the gorgeous woman in front of him. He let his hands roam up over her legs, gently squeezing and kneading the flesh as he traveled. When he got to her inner thighs, she trembled beneath his touches, but he didn't stop.

Seth traced one finger around the elastic of her panties; her little sounds of anticipation caused his dick to grow even harder in his shorts. He desperately wanted to slide his fingers past the elastic and directly to her core, and he knew she wanted that too, but he continued his travel up her body until he reached her flat stomach. He spread out his large hands on her belly. It was firm and flat with just enough womanly softness and his hands spanned her. He connected his fingers in a diamond over her belly button and kissed her stomach.

There was a baby in there. *His baby.* The thought slammed into him. Soon her perfectly flat stomach would grow and swell as her child—*his child*—he took a breath—their child grew.

It wasn't quite panic that filled him at the idea, but something else. Something he couldn't put his finger on. Under his hands, Cynthia breathed hard; her chest rose and fell, her breasts heaving with every breath.

When he looked up, there were tears in her eyes and a look on her face he couldn't read. "Cynthia, don't cry. It's going to be—"

"Don't talk," she whispered. "Please. Just…just make love to me."

———

CYNTHIA HADN'T HAD a long time to imagine any of the scenarios that could have played out when they finally got their test results. But even in the short time she'd had to think about it, she'd certainly never imagined Seth's reaction to finding out he was going to be a father would be to seduce her. More than that, she never would have guessed that not only would it be okay with her, it would be exactly what she needed.

But when he touched her stomach and then kissed it, it was too much. She could see it in his eyes, too. But now that they'd started, she needed it. More than she knew, she needed him to love her. Even if it wasn't real. She needed for at least a few minutes to believe that the baby she was carrying wasn't a mistake.

"Make love to me," she repeated.

The desire she thought might be gone flared in his eyes again and he brought his body up, supporting his weight with his forearms on either side of her so he all but covered her. He didn't say a word, but kissed her with so much tenderness and passion that it almost broke her again. But she wouldn't let it. Instead, she reached up and pulled him into her, kissing him harder. Her hips ground against his; the hard length of him pressed into her and he moaned low and sexy.

"Seth, I need you."

He growled in response, which was all the agreement she needed. With one hand, he managed to tug her panties down, and Cynthia wriggled out of them before she pulled at his underpants and freed him.

He kissed her again, but it ended too soon. "Dammit."

She opened her eyes. "What?"

"I don't have a condom."

The first thought was one of shock. *Seth McBride didn't have a condom in his apartment? That wasn't very responsible of him.* Her next thought surprised her with the reality of it. "I don't think that's really an issue anymore, do you?"

She watched his eyes light up in acknowledgment. He shook his head and as she watched his eyes darkened with desire as he raised himself up over her. And then with one thrust he was inside her, filling her. Cynthia squeezed her eyes shut and he stilled, letting her grow used to him.

When she opened her eyes again, he stared right at her. Normally, she'd want to look away from the intimate moment, but she couldn't. He moved inside her and with every thrust, the pressure in her core built, the intensity of the moment increasing until finally she couldn't take it anymore. She closed her eyes and gave herself over to the release as she came completely undone. Without the condom barrier between them, she felt the intensity of his release as well.

For a few blissful moments, there was nothing to focus on except for the overwhelming orgasm as it crashed through her body, filling her with wave after wave of intensity.

All too soon, the light feeling floated away and she came back to herself with the reality of her situation hitting her harder than before. Only now it was worse because Seth knew and his reaction hadn't been to run or scream or say hurtful things. He hadn't even collapsed to the couch with his head in his hands, contemplating the end of life as he knew it. He hadn't done any of those things. No, instead he'd made love to her. And that's what it was, too. At least that's what it felt like to her. It was more than just a hookup. But probably not to him. He was likely just dealing with stress the only way he knew how. After all, wasn't that Seth's MO?

It had felt so right, but Cynthia knew deep down it wasn't. Things with Seth—the entire situation—it was all so far from *right.* She couldn't open her eyes right away, afraid she'd cry again. Only now she knew if he saw her tears, he'd be concerned and want to know what was wrong.

But there was no way she could answer him if he asked. After all, how could she when the answer was both *I don't know* and *everything*?

When she finally had a handle on her emotions, or at least enough to trust that she wouldn't burst out into tears, she opened her eyes to see him watching her quizzically.

"Cynthia?" He brushed the hair off her face with a touch so gentle, she almost lost the tentative grip on her control. "Are you…I mean, I don't really know what the proper reaction in this situation is, but I just needed to—"

"It's okay." She smiled at his clumsy way with words. "I get it. I totally get it." She felt another wave of emotion, and before she could worry about tears, she slid out from under him and grabbed up her clothes. "Just give me a minute, okay?"

He didn't protest and she didn't look back, but headed for the bathroom to clean up and pull herself together.

The minute she closed the door behind her and leaned back against it, she realized her mistake. The three pregnancy tests, all with positive answers, were directly in front of her to give her yet another stark reminder of her reality.

She was going to be a mother.

And Seth was going to be a father.

Whether she liked it or not, they were in it together. Only she wasn't naive enough to think that they'd actually be together. What they'd shared might have felt like more to her, but she wasn't dumb enough to think it was anything more for Seth. Nor was she naive enough to think there ever would be. Seth would never change and even if he did, that didn't mean he was the right man for her.

Her hand went to her stomach and the life that grew inside there.

"I'm sorry, baby," she whispered. "I haven't made very good choices. But I promise that I'll do better. For you." She thought for a moment and looked at her reflection in the mirror before she added, "For both of us."

WHEN SHE WAS DRESSED and her emotions were firmly in check, Cynthia took a deep breath and went back out to the living room when what she really wanted to do was slip out a window and run home without facing him. She might have, too, if she hadn't left her shoes and jacket in the main room.

"Hey," she said, finding Seth waiting on the couch. He jumped up when she walked in. "I'm going to get going." She moved quickly and grabbed her coat. "It's been kind of a long day and I think I should get some—"

"Don't you think we should talk?"

She shook her head. "I don't think there's much to talk about at this point."

"Are you kidding? There's quite a bit to discuss." He'd managed to move himself between her and the door as if he knew she'd make her escape given half the chance.

Cynthia took a breath and exhaled slowly. "Look, Seth. It was a mistake."

"What was a mistake? This?" He waved his hand between them. "Or the time before? Or the time before that?"

She blanched at his words, but her resolve only steeled. "This time. Last time...yes. All of it." She tried not to notice his reaction, the surprise in his eyes. "Look, you might deal with your problems by having sex and hoping they go away, but this isn't going to just go away."

"You think that's what I was doing?" He stepped toward her, and instinctively, she shrank back against the wall. "You thought getting you naked and underneath me would somehow make me forget about the fact that you're pregnant with my child. A child who will be part of me forever. Really? Why wouldn't a little fucking make it all go away, right?"

She flinched at his choice of words but mostly with what they implied.

"May I remind you that you were there, too?" He looked at her pointedly. "In fact, you were an active and dare I say, willing participant to this *problem-solving sex.*"

Cynthia felt her face flush, but that only made her angrier. She took a step forward and put a hand on his chest to push past him. "I'm not doing this, Seth."

"Doing what?"

She took a deep breath and stared him in the eyes. "I'm not going to pretend that just because we're having a baby together that we're going to be anything more. I don't expect that. I wasn't trying to trap you or anything. I know what kind of guy you are."

"Oh yeah?" He crossed his arms over his chest. "And what kind is that?"

She shook her head and turned away. "I'm not doing this," she repeated.

"I think we're already doing it." He spun her around. "Finish it."

His eyes challenged her to just say what she was thinking. "Fine." She rose to the challenge. "You're not the relationship type and I don't expect that to change, just because of this." Her hand lightly fluttered to her belly but didn't rest there. "You're a player; it's all you've ever been." He blinked hard, and she pretended not to see the hurt in his eyes. "I'm leaving."

To her surprise, he let her pass. "Leaving won't solve this, Cynthia."

"No. But it'll get me away from you." She spat her words at him, wanting to hurt him.

She grabbed her tote bag and tugged her shoes on. As she moved for the door, he was there, blocking her way. She didn't want to look at him, but with his still naked chest only inches from her, she had no choice but to look up into his face. His eyes blazed with heat and anger, but when he spoke his voice held no edge. "Go if you need to. But before you do, know this…" He used his thumb to stroke a soft, smooth circle on her cheek. "Tonight? It wasn't about forgetting, Cynthia. It was about remembering."

His words washed through her but before she could respond, he was gone, giving her space to leave.

And not knowing what else to do—she did.

Chapter Six

WITH MALCOLM OUT OF TOWN, the hill was Seth's responsibility. It was happening more and more lately that Malcolm was gone, and he knew it would be like that at least for the next few years because Malcolm couldn't stand the idea of being away from Kylie for more than a few days at a time. But Seth didn't mind; in fact, he welcomed the increased workload over the last week. It helped take his mind off the fact that he was going to be a father and that the mother of that child seemed to think he was a womanizing man whore who couldn't possibly deal with anything serious in his life. At least that was the message she'd been sending. And he'd received it loud and clear. Especially since he hadn't heard from or seen her since the night she left his apartment after he'd basically told her that their time together had actually meant something to him—hell, that *she* meant something to him.

At least that's what he thought he'd told her. Women were so damn complicated.

Seth pounded the tall red pole into the hill. It was the last gate for the ski race course, and just in time, too. He could hear the kids at the top of the hill, gathering with their coach for a practice run. Seth waved up to them, picked up his mallet and headed to the edge of the ski run where he'd left his skis.

He still had office work to do, but it could wait. The conditions on the hill were great and he'd happily spend his entire day crossing things off his to-do list outside before he had to head in.

And maybe sneak in a run or two for fun, too. Which is exactly what he was headed to do. Some hard-hitting moguls would help take his mind off Cynthia and the baby. Maybe he'd even get some clarity as to how to get her to talk to him again. Never mind talk about the baby and how exactly they were going to handle things.

He was just about to ski off, when he caught a flash of red, followed by a spray of snow, as Marcus came to an impressive stop on his snowboard next to him.

"Hey, man. I've been looking for you everywhere." Marcus was barely out of breath despite what had to have been a grueling run down the hill. He was one of the best snowboarders around. In fact, he was the best snowboarder in Cedar Springs and likely all of western North America. He'd been on the pro circuit for a while before returning home for his twin brother's grand opening of Stone Summit.

Seth had always liked Marcus, even if they hadn't really gotten to know each other very well. At any rate, it was good to have him around again. Though Seth did have to wonder why he'd give up the snowboarding circuit to settle back into life in a small town. "I've been working double time." Seth clicked his boots into his bindings.

"That's right." Marcus pulled his goggles up onto his helmet. "You know, if my brother would hire some more help around here, it wouldn't be so bad. He really does need a manager."

"Settle down, buddy. That's my job."

"Well, maybe an assistant manager then."

Seth narrowed his eyes at the other man. Was he really considering giving up his boarding career to be an assistant manager at his brother's hill? He'd ask him about it, but not now. The middle of the hill was not the place to have such a conversation. Besides, there was clearly something else on his mind.

"What were you needing to talk to me about?"

"Why don't we finish this run and talk about it on the chair going up?" Marcus pulled his goggles back into place. "Assuming you have time for a little break." He winked and with a flip of his board, took off with Seth in hard pursuit.

Seth pushed himself to keep up to Marcus's boarding skills. Marcus was a professional for sure, but Seth was no slouch either, and they fell into a rhythm as they raced down the hill. When they were settled onto the chair lift, Seth got right down to it. "What's up?"

"I need your help."

"I figured as much."

"Seriously, though." Marcus did look serious. Very serious, so Seth sat up and paid attention. "I want to do something for Kylie."

"Oh no." Seth held up a gloved hand and shook his head. It was no secret that Marcus and Kylie used to date, long before Malcolm was in the picture. It was also no secret that Marcus had made a clumsy and somewhat obvious attempt to break them up again. Sort of. It was complicated. Which was exactly why Seth wanted absolutely nothing to do with it. He had enough *complicated* on his own. He didn't need Marcus's too. "Whatever it is, leave me out of it."

"It's not like that."

"Don't care." Seth looked away.

"Don't be a jackass." Marcus punched Seth's arm. "I'm not trying to get her back or anything. I'm trying to do something nice."

"Nice?" Seth narrowed his eyes and lifted his goggles so he could get a better look at his friend, but there was nothing but sincerity in the other man's face. "I'm listening."

"Well, as you might know, there have been issues between us in the past." Seth almost laughed, but Marcus looked so serious, he swallowed it back. "I thought it might be a good show of faith to throw Kylie a party. Kind of a going away, we're really proud of you, party."

"A party? Really?"

"Really."

"And what's in it for you?" Seth felt bad assuming that Marcus had an angle, but then again, he knew Marcus.

"Honestly?"

Seth nodded.

"Nothing."

The chair crested the last rise before the top of the hill and the men prepared to disembark. The break gave Seth a moment to think. It would be a nice thing for Kylie to have a going-away party. Her leaving and preparation for nursing school had been quite disjointed as they'd gone back and forth between Vancouver and Cedar Springs. But soon, she'd be gone pretty much until summer. Seth skied off the chair and waited for Marcus under the large wooden area map. When Marcus joined him, Seth had come to a decision.

"I think it sounds like a good idea," he said.

Marcus smiled and he looked so much like his twin brother it caught Seth off guard.

"But there better not be any hidden agenda," Seth added, still unable to totally trust Marcus's intentions. "No offense."

Marcus laughed. "None taken. I mean it when I say I want to do something nice. I was a jerk. Hell, I've been a jerk most of the time I've known her. My brother loves her, which means it would be better if she didn't hate me in return."

"And there's the angle." Seth smiled and shook his head.

"But as far as angles go, it's a pretty good one. We'll figure something out. We can do the party up here in the lodge. But for now, I have enough time for one more quick run and then I really have to get back to work."

"Deal." Marcus bent down and strapped his foot onto his board. "Try to keep up this time."

SHE'D HAD a few days to think about it. Two days to process her new reality. But it didn't matter whether Cynthia had two days or two years; she was pretty sure she'd never be fully able to process exactly what type of mess she'd gotten herself into. She was going to be a mother and it couldn't have happened at a worse time. Or with a worse guy.

No. That wasn't true. It wasn't true at all. Seth wasn't a bad guy. He just wasn't the right guy for her. Despite the way her traitorous body reacted whenever she thought about him. She had to be responsible and part of that was figuring out what felt right and what *was* right. And getting involved with a man like Seth, even if he was the father of her child—okay, *especially* because he was the father of her child—was not right.

She'd avoided the ski hill, which meant she hadn't seen Nala or the puppies in almost a week. They were probably getting so big and starting to walk around. Maybe even venturing out of their box a bit. The maintenance shed didn't seem like the safest place for a litter of newborn puppies. At least that's how she rationalized the decision to go up the hill and visit them. Besides, she had Colton working the store until closing, which meant she had the afternoon and evening off and there was nothing else to do. Except, of course, tell her mom that she was going to be a grandmother.

Cynthia shuddered at the thought, grabbed her car keys and made the easy choice to put off facing reality. At least for a few more hours. The drive to the hill was easy and only took a few minutes. Despite the snow still up high in the mountains, most of the snow down in Cedar Springs was melted; the ice on the lake had started to break up and the roads were clear. It was easy to be fooled into thinking that spring was just around the corner, but Cynthia knew better. There'd be at least one more big dump of snow, maybe even two, and the ski season would go well into April.

If the town below looked like the early stages of spring, as Cynthia got closer to Stone Summit, it was easy to see that winter was still very much in the mountains. She left her car in the parking lot and pulled her coat tight around her as she made her way through the ski hill village. Stone Summit was still a work in progress, and she knew Malcolm had big plans for the development, but he also had a vision to keep the base of the hill a small, cozy village. Right now it consisted of the rental shop and the lodge, which had a cafeteria, bar for après ski drinks, and a coffee bar. A small building next to the lodge housed the main offices; some private chalets off to the side backed onto the ski hill so the residents could ski right from their door; and of course, the maintenance shed was tucked behind all of the main buildings.

It was getting to the end of the day and people milled about as they finished off their skiing for the day. No doubt there were people in the crowd who Cynthia knew, which was exactly why she snuck around the back of the buildings. She hadn't felt much like small talk for the last few days and she sucked at keeping secrets. Even if they were her own. She also didn't want to have to explain herself or her behavior at the Paw the other night, and she knew without a doubt that there was more than one person who was dying to ask her about it. It was best she just avoid talking to people in general. At least until she sorted herself out.

The door to the shed was closed, which she hoped meant

Seth wasn't there. She made her way through the dim building until she got to the back corner. Nala lifted her head to greet her and wagged her tail against the blankets while her pups nursed.

"Hey, girl." Cynthia knelt next to the box and scratched the dog's head. It had been about a week, but she still recognized Cynthia and was clearly happy to see her. Of course, it must get lonely as a new mother with no one to keep you company while you took care of your babies.

Oh God.

Would that be her? Would she be all alone while she took care of her new baby? The thought hit her hard and fast and didn't make any sense at all. It was ridiculous. Carmen and Dylan, who ran the Springs resort, had a baby not too long ago and they were out and about. In fact, Carmen was always taking her son to classes and carrying him around in a sling contraption while she worked. Or at least she did when he was little; he had to be almost a toddler now. How did Carmen manage now? How would she manage?

Cynthia forced herself to take a deep breath. She was getting ahead of herself. In a big way. She was a strong, capable woman. She'd figure it out. And she'd ask Carmen for some tips, too.

As the puppies finished their snack, they wiggled around and crawled over one another and their mother. They'd grown so quickly and were a lot more active than the last time Cynthia had been to check on them. She picked up the white one that had a trace of black around her eyes. The puppy licked her hand and then her nose, and Cynthia laughed.

She nuzzled the impossibly soft fur. "You're so cute."

"So are you."

She froze for a second before she put the puppy down. She'd known there'd be a risk of running into Seth. A big one. And she'd be lying if she said that wasn't partly why she'd decided to make the trip up the hill. "Hi, Seth." She didn't bother to turn around, but focused on picking up another puppy. After all, they should all get equal attention.

This one was darker than the first one, with a lot more black on his head and paws. "Aren't you a handsome little guy?"

"Thank you." Seth chuckled behind her. "But I wouldn't say I'm little."

She appreciated his attempt to lighten the mood, even if it was lame. At least it was something. She knew they needed to talk, but she'd dreaded it ever since she'd stormed out of his apartment. Mostly because of the tension between them. Tension she knew she was responsible for.

"I'm sorry," she said softly.

"For calling me little?" He crouched next to her.

"No. And you know it."

"I'm sorry, too." His voice had lost the teasing edge. She turned to look at him, the puppy still in her hand. "Can we start over?"

She laughed and rubbed the puppy's head before she put him back in the box with the others. "It's a little late for that, don't you think?"

"In some respects, certainly." Seth touched her arm in a move that was completely unexpected and sweet. "But I meant as far as this situation goes. I don't want to start out on this... well, journey for lack of a better word...fighting. There's no point to it."

Not only was he right, it was an incredibly insightful thing to say and she hadn't expected it out of him. He was surprising her more and more, it seemed. "You're right." She nodded. "There's no point fighting. I don't want to be one of those angry baby mamas."

Seth burst out laughing. "You could never be one of those angry baby mamas."

"Don't be so sure. I've been an emotional nightmare these last few weeks. I don't think I've ever cried so much in my whole life."

Cynthia picked up the third pup, partly because she didn't want him to feel left out, but mostly because she needed a distraction from Seth. "I can't believe how big they're getting." She changed the subject completely.

"I know." He reached out and picked up the other two puppies, trying with limited success to contain them both on his lap. "They'll need homes soon."

Automatically, Cynthia looked at Nala. How would the mother dog react to being separated from her babies? How would the puppies bear it? Logically, she knew dogs were different than humans, but still—the idea of having her baby taken away from her…well, she just couldn't think about it. She nuzzled the puppy's furry head. Unfortunately, she did have the misfortune of thinking about things from the puppies' perspective ever since her mother had gotten sick. It was a reality that her mother would be taken from her soon. And sure, it was different, but still.

Tears sprang to her eyes and she wiped at them angrily before Seth could notice.

"Wow," he said. "You weren't kidding. You are emotional."

She smacked his arm lightly at his teasing. "Like you hadn't already noticed."

He laughed and put the puppies he was holding back in the box before he took the little one out of her hands and put him with his siblings. "I think you should have a puppy."

That dried up her tears. "Are you kidding me?"

"Not at all. It's kind of symbolic, really. I mean, the puppies and Valentine's Day and…you and me." He shrugged. "Which one do you want?"

He was crazy. Absolutely certifiable. And she told him so. "Seth, why the hell would I want to deal with a puppy and all the work that goes with it? Don't you think I'm going to have enough to keep me busy in a few months?"

She watched as realization crossed his face before she nodded knowingly and gave him a look.

"Right. I just thought—"

"It's fine." An idea came to her and she rolled it around in her head for a second before she spoke. "What about Nala?"

"What about her?" Seth scratched the mother dog's head. "She'll need a home, too, I guess."

"You're not keeping her?"

"My place is hardly big enough for a husky."

"I want her." She blurted it out before she could change her mind, although she knew she wouldn't. She'd felt a connection to the mother dog from the first night she met her. Besides, it seemed right…two single mothers living together.

"I thought you said you were going to have enough to deal with? Which is true," he added quickly. "I mean, I know you'll have a lot to deal with and—"

"But she's not a puppy. I won't have to worry about all that training and puppy stuff. Besides, I think we belong together." Nala looked up and licked Cynthia's hand as if she understood exactly what was happening.

"I think it's a good idea." Something in Seth's voice didn't sound totally convinced.

"But what?"

His face transformed as he gave her a sexy and somewhat mischievous grin. "Well, technically, she's my dog. So really, I should—"

"You just said—"

"I know what I said, but it's true."

She glared at him and knew her face was likely turning a bright shade of red.

"But I'm willing to work something out," he added with a devilish grin.

She knew she'd regret asking, but she did anyway. "What?"

"Date me."

If he'd told her he was a direct descendant of an alien from Mars she couldn't have been more surprised. In fact, that would have made more sense. "Pardon me?"

"Date me," he repeated. "We kind of skipped that step in all this and I think we should give it a try. Let me take you for dinner, go see a movie, maybe even go skiing." He shrugged. "You know, date things. Date me, and you can have Nala."

"That's crazy." She struggled to wrap her brain around what he said. Date him? Seth didn't date. He was a chronic bachelor. Everyone knew that.

"It's not crazy at all." He pinned her with his gaze and challenged her with his eyes. "We're going to have a baby together, aren't we? Why is it crazy to date?"

"You don't date."

"That's not true." He reached for her hand. "I just haven't found anyone worth dating. Until now."

Damn if her heart didn't do a little flip at his words. Stupid pregnancy hormones. And it had to be hormones. She didn't have anything else to blame for the way she felt when he looked at her that way. Never mind when he touched her like that. It must be some sort of natural response because she was carrying his child.

"I don't get it," she said slowly, measuring her words in an effort to sort through her feelings as she spoke. "Shouldn't you be freaking out? I mean, isn't that the natural response to finding out you accidentally knocked up a one-night stand, ending life as you know it and completely ruining your future?"

He squeezed her hand and pulled her a little bit closer before he answered. "First of all, it wasn't a one-night stand." His grin made her heart skip in a totally cliché way. "Second of all, I am freaking out a little bit because I wouldn't be human if I wasn't. But just so you know, yes, it was an accident. But this"—he laid a hand on her stomach, over her jacket—"and you, have in no way ruined my life. It's just different. So what do you say? Date me?"

Cynthia held his eyes as he spoke and absorbed his touch through her thick jacket before she answered the only way she possibly could. "Yes."

Chapter Seven

SETH WALKED her out of the shed and watched as Cynthia got into her car and headed down the mountain. He managed to hold himself together until he was sure she'd driven out of sight. Then he bent and put his hands on his knees in an effort to suck air into his lungs and his obviously oxygen-deprived brain.

Hell yes, he was freaking out. Cynthia had asked, and he'd done his best to pretend to be calm and collected about everything, but on the inside he was a total mess. For the last few days, he'd managed to neatly compartmentalize his feelings and focus on work and pretty much everything else besides the fact that he would be a totally unplanned father. It likely wasn't the healthiest way to cope, but it was a method that mostly seemed to be working. At least until he saw Cynthia. That made everything crystal-clear. He was going to be a father.

Shit.

Not that he was unhappy about it. There were feelings of anxiety, for sure. He was scared and a bit confused. But in a strange, totally surprising way, he was kind of happy about it. He was going to be a father.

Sure, it wasn't the way he'd planned to become a father. Not that he'd ever really given it much thought before. But something about the situation, no matter how screwed up it was, felt kind of right, too. And on the plus side, Cynthia had agreed to date him. And that idea made him happier than anything else at the moment.

He'd never planned to make any kind of deal with her about the dog. Hell, he would have happily given Nala to Cynthia. But when the opportunity presented itself, it seemed like a good way to get her to spend time with him and hopefully during that time he could somehow convince her that he wasn't just a womanizing player and that there might actually be more to him. Because there was and he hadn't been lying when he told her that he'd been waiting for someone worth dating to come along.

Seth straightened up and let the cold air fill his lungs.

He was just about to go lock up the office and head down to the Grizzly Paw, where maybe Samantha would be willing to give him some tips on dating considering it was more than a little out of his wheelhouse, when his cell phone chirped to alert him to a text message.

It was Malcolm.

STUCK IN VANCOUVER. *Need you to meet with Trent.*

SETH SHOOK HIS HEAD. He'd been looking forward to an evening off but it didn't look like that was going to happen. He couldn't blame the guy—he was in love—but why set a meeting with Trent, the manager of the Springs resort, while he was out of town? It didn't make sense. Not that it had to. Seth quickly typed a message in return.

· · ·

STUCK? Or staying? Why make a meeting while you're out of town?

THE REPLY CAME QUICKLY.

A LAST-MINUTE THING. Final details about the spring ski packages. Can you do it?

SETH SHOOK his head but he knew he'd do it. Trent and Malcolm had been working together on some "stay and ski" package deals for guests of the resort to enjoy the ski hill. Nothing had been finalized for the season, but Seth knew how important it was to get a jump on these things. With the inaugural season of Stone Summit winding down in the next six weeks, it was more important than ever.

NO PROBLEM, he typed back and then turned around to grab his things from his office before he headed over to the resort.

IT WAS TIME. No, Cynthia corrected herself. It was past time.

She needed to tell her mom about the baby. Maybe it would even cheer her up? Jess said her mom had been down lately and not feeling very good. Not that one could ever feel better when you had terminal cancer. But there were definitely good and bad days. She just hoped the news of a grandchild would help with the good days.

"It'll be okay." Jess, who was just organizing her things before she headed home for the day, noticed Cynthia's hesitation. "She'll be happy to hear about it. Especially if you're happy about it," she said pointedly.

"I am happy." Cynthia's hand flew to her stomach. She'd told Jess the truth the night she'd taken the tests. Mostly because Jess already suspected, but also because she'd needed to talk to someone besides Seth, who didn't seem very interested in talking at all and Kylie wasn't around. "I am," she said again. "I'm just scared."

Jess smiled kindly and squeezed her arm. "Of course you are. I would be worried if you weren't. But it will be okay. And your mom will be thrilled. Go share it with her. I'll see you tomorrow, okay?"

Cynthia nodded and forced a small smile. She waited until she heard the door click shut; she picked up the tray of tea and crackers she'd already set out and walked down the hall.

"Mom?" She tapped lightly on the door with the back of her hand and shifted the tray so she could open the door. "Are you awake?"

Her mom was propped up on her bed in a nest of pillows. Her eyes were closed, but then she opened her mouth. "I am." She managed a weak smile and it almost broke Cynthia's heart. Her mother had once been vibrant and full of life. As a single mother who also ran a business, Linda had been a force in Cedar Springs. But she was so frail now—a shadow of who she used to be—and it had all happened so quickly.

Cynthia moved across the room and put the tray down on the table next to the bed. "How are you feeling?" It was a stupid question, but nonetheless, it was the only stupid question Cynthia couldn't seem to quit asking.

It was also the only question her mother refused to answer outright. "Come sit with me," Linda said. "Jess said you weren't feeling well. Are you working too hard?"

Cynthia smiled and tucked herself onto the edge of her mother's bed. Even on her sickbed, she couldn't stop fussing over her. It was a trait that used to make Cynthia crazy, especially as a teenager when she'd gone through her wild phase. Now it just made her kind of sad. Who would worry about her when her mother passed?

"I'm not working too hard, Mom." She felt a twinge of guilt for not immediately addressing the situation, but quickly rationalized it with the fact that she didn't want to shock her too badly. But really, she was just a terrible coward. "I have Colton. Remember him? He's a good kid and he's been a lot of help in the shop. But I suppose he'll be graduating this summer, so I should probably look at hiring someone else." Cynthia was aware that she was rambling, but it always helped to talk about all the mundane things that filled her days and normally her mother liked to hear all the boring details, too. But something was off today. Cynthia stopped talking and looked carefully at her mother. "Are you okay, Mom? Honestly. You look…different."

"I was wondering the same thing about you." Her mother deflected the question easily. "Tell me what's really going on with you." She reached out and placed her hand on Cynthia's.

Cynthia scooped it up in her own and stared down at the thin skin that covered her mother's frail hand. A hand that soothed so many of her bumps and scrapes over the years. The very same hand that she held on her first day of kindergarten as she walked to her class. The hand that pulled her into a tight hug the day she graduated from high school.

The very same hand her unborn child would never get a chance to hold.

She didn't realize she was crying until her mother spoke. "Talk to me, honey. What's going on?"

Cynthia cradled her mother's hand as gently as she could and looked into her eyes. They were so full of pain and exhaustion, but they were still the same kind eyes she knew so well.

She licked her dry lips and tried to sound as calm as possible when she said, "I'm going to have a baby, Mom."

She didn't know how her mom would react. To be fair, Cynthia hadn't put much thought into her mother's response, only the act of actually telling her. A deep silence filled the room and Cynthia had to check to see that her mother hadn't fallen asleep. She hadn't. Linda stared at her, unblinking.

"Mom? Did you hear me?"

She nodded but still didn't speak.

Cynthia's tears dried up and she stroked small circles on the back of her mom's hand for a few minutes while she waited for her to speak. Finally, she couldn't bear the silence anymore.

"Mom?" Linda blinked and her eyes focused on her daughter. "Do you have any questions? Or...well...anything to say?"

She nodded slowly. "I have a lot of things to say. And of course I have questions."

"Ask me anything."

Cynthia braced herself for the list of questions she was sure her mother would have for her. Things like: How far along are you? When did you find out? Who's the father?

The last one would be the hardest to handle, but she'd deal with it. Now that she was actually sitting here with her mother and the truth was out, albeit with less than an enthusiastic reception, she was eager to answer some of the questions and actually *talk* about the baby for the first time.

Linda opened her mouth and closed it again before she spoke. When she finally did, tears swam in her eyes. "Why would you tell me such a thing?"

THE SPRINGS RESORT was set slightly down the mountain from Stone Summit and it only took Seth ten minutes to get there and park his car. Walking through the front doors never failed to impress him. The resort was posh for sure, but it was far from pretentious. Everyone felt instantly at ease when they walked through the front doors. Whether they were wearing blue jeans or the finest designer suit, the Springs had an almost magical restorative quality that just made people relax.

Water was everywhere, even flowing outside under the bridge Seth walked over on his way inside. Steam rose off the water because it came directly from the natural hot springs that fed the therapeutic waters of the resort. He took a deep breath, closed his eyes and let his senses fill with the relaxation that washed over him as he stood in the lobby.

"Feeling Zen today, are you?"

He opened his eyes to see Carmen Kincaid, the customer service manager at the Springs and also a good friend. Seth opened his arms for a hug, and she complied.

"It's good to see you, Carmen. It's been too long. What's new?"

She laughed and her smile lit up her face. Carmen was always so warm and friendly. Nothing ever seemed to get her down. "It's been crazy around here with little Hunter, and managing everything. But we're figuring it out."

"Of course you are." Seth smiled and made a mental note to talk to Dylan, Carmen's boyfriend and Hunter's father, about what fatherhood was really like. He knew he'd be able to get some tips from the man. But not yet. He couldn't even be sure whether Cynthia was ready to tell anyone. He still wasn't sure of much. He shook his head and refocused on the reason he was there. "I'm supposed to be meeting Trent. Is he around? Apparently Malcolm had a meeting but he got caught in the city and...well, you know how it goes."

"I do. They have a lot on their plate right now. It's good of you to help Malcolm out while he focuses on Kylie. I know they both must appreciate it so much." She smiled again and gestured through the lobby. "I think Trent is in the Stillwater, having a bite to eat. Jax wanted him to try some new recipes."

They walked together through the lobby. "Sounds like I showed up at the right time." His stomach growled at the idea of tasting some of Jax Carver's creations. As the head chef at the Stillwater, he was second to none and they were all lucky to have him and his food so close.

"I'm sure there'll be enough for you, too." Carmen chuckled. "I'll let you find your own way there. I have a few things to take care of at the desk here."

Seth gave Carmen a peck on the cheek with promises to get together soon, although both of them knew with their busy schedules it likely wouldn't happen for quite some time, and Seth headed down to the restaurant.

"LOOKS GOOD, CARVER." Seth gave the chef a friendly smack on the back as he slipped into the booth across from Trent. "Don't suppose you have a bit for me to try?"

Jax turned around and gave Seth a smile that didn't quite reach his eyes. The two men weren't close friends like so many others in town. Mostly they just hadn't had much of a chance to get to know each other, but then there was the small detail that Jax used to hook up with Cynthia and even though he'd never been serious with her—at least not before—it had never sat right with Seth.

"You know it, man," Jax said companionably. "I was actually going to head back into the kitchen to get the next dish. I'll fix you a plate?"

"Sounds great." He waited for Jax to leave before he turned his attention to Trent. "Hey. I know you were probably expecting Malcolm, but—"

"Nah. He texted me and told me you were coming. It's good to see you. How are things over at the hill?"

They fell into an easy back and forth about their respective businesses and the talk naturally shifted to the reason for their meeting. Trent pulled out a portfolio and slid a piece of paper across the table to Seth. "This is what we're proposing for a spring ski package."

Seth scanned the numbers. "So we'll cut our ticket price by twenty percent?"

"And we'll cut our room rate by ten percent and throw in a coupon for a free thirty-minute massage."

Seth raised his eyebrows and quickly crunched a few numbers in his head. Spring was a notoriously tricky season for a ski hill. There could be a huge dump of snow, extending the season or...not. Meaning, the hill would struggle to stay open until the end of April, which would be the ideal closing time. Especially for a brand new hill. A lot was riding on the spring season. Making a "Stay and Ski" deal with the Springs would guarantee pre-booking and ticket sales. Even at the discount, it would be a good thing. "I'll tell you what, we'll also throw in fifteen percent off lessons and rentals."

"Nice." Trent nodded and made a note on the paper. "I think we can do a good business with this. I know where you're at with Stone Summit and I'll tell you, the more we can attract guests to the resort, the better we all are. The way I see it, it's win-win." He extended his hand and Seth happily shook on it. He probably should have run it past Malcolm first, but Seth also knew that was the reason Malcolm had hired him in the first place. He didn't need nor did he want to be pestered with all the little details. Besides, there was absolutely nothing wrong with this plan.

"And just in time for the Slush Cup."

"I keep hearing about this Slush Cup," Trent said. "What exactly is it?"

Seth leaned back in his chair and smiled. This was where he excelled. He might be new to the idea of organizing promotions and sales plans, but when it came to fun on the ski hill, he had that down pat. "It's going to be great and I think it could become a tradition at Stone Summit," he started to explain. "Basically, it'll be a party to shut down the ski season. We'll build a pool at the base of the hill and—"

"A pool?" Trent cocked his head and looked at him dubiously. "At a ski hill? That makes no sense."

"It makes a lot of sense." Seth smiled. "Hear me out." Trent nodded and Seth continued. "So we'll build a pool, which won't be too hard since we have such a thick base of snow." Trent didn't look convinced, but Seth continued anyway, confident in his idea. "Anyway, we build a little jump at the lip of the pool and people ski down, go off the jump and land in the water."

"Seriously?"

Seth grinned. "Absolutely. But that's not the best part."

"Really?"

"They compete for prizes like biggest splash, best faceplant, and most creative costume."

"Wait." Trent held up his hand. "There are costumes?"

"Of course. There has to be costumes." He shrugged. "We'll bring in some live music, maybe some beer gardens and hype it as a big fun day. Oh, and all the entry fees can go to a charity."

"Hmm..."

"Sounds good, doesn't it?"

"It actually does," Trent agreed. "Where did you come up with this idea?"

"It's not totally my idea," Seth admitted. "I read about something like it done at a hill in Europe and I've always thought it would be the perfect type of thing to bring to Cedar Springs and now, Stone Summit. You know how the community likes to get involved in things."

"They do." Trent nodded his agreement. "We do." He

slapped his hand on the table as one of the waitresses brought out two plates and placed them in front of the men before she briefly explained that it was a chicken curry with jasmine rice. The aroma made Seth's mouth water and both men tucked into the plates before Trent spoke again. "I like it, McBride. Malcolm's on board with it?"

"In theory." Seth shrugged and took another bite. "We spoke about it briefly but never really had time to hash out the details. I was going to take it on as my personal project." That was before he found out about another little, more pressing personal project he'd have to deal with when it came to Cynthia. But he'd make it work.

"Well, I think it sounds like a lot of fun. What date are you looking at? I assume you have a band lined up and everything in order for the beer gardens?"

Trent's questions took him off guard. He didn't actually have a lot of the details worked out. "End of April. The twenty-fifth." He started with the one detail he was sure on. "That's closing day. I don't actually have a band. I was thinking of asking Slade, but I think we need more of a band rather than a one-man act."

"Agreed. If you want me to, I'll check with the Jacked Crackers. They like playing small towns and something like this would be right up their alley."

The Jacked Crackers played the summer solstice festival in Cedar Springs awhile back, which was the first time Slade Black came to town, which planted the seed that ultimately led to him returning and falling in love with Beth, which sparked a solo career. Or the other way around—Seth could never remember. Either way, the Jacked Crackers had since recovered from the loss of their lead guitar player and were on fire in the rock world. If Trent could get them to play, it would be a big draw.

"That would be fantastic," Seth agreed. "And although we

have a liquor license up at the hill, I thought maybe Samantha and Grizzly Paw would like in on it, too. We could split things and she could provide the staff."

"You can talk to her about that." Trent shook his head and stuffed another forkful into his mouth. "Don't get me wrong," he said after a moment. "It's not that I don't think it's a good idea, but Samantha's been run off her feet lately. She seriously needs to hire some more staff. I know she wants to have kids one day, but if she keeps working the way she does, we'll never be able to—and...why am I telling you this?"

Seth smiled. The other man clearly had something on his mind and if he needed to unload on someone, Seth was more than okay with it. Especially if it took his mind off everything in his own life. "It's okay, man. I have that effect on people." They both laughed but Trent's died quickly.

"Seriously. Can I just say one thing? And then I promise I'll shut up."

Seth nodded and took another bite of the amazing curry.

"She wants to start a family." Seth almost choked on the rice. *Was there something going around with the women in town and babies?* "Which is fine," Trent continued. "More than fine. It's great. But, it's not as easy as you might think."

Seth had to shovel in another bite to keep him from telling Trent that sometimes it was easier than you wanted it to be. Somehow he didn't think that would be the right thing to say at that moment.

"Anyway, it's hard on a relationship," Trent said. "Kind of takes the fun out of it, ya know?"

He didn't, but Seth nodded anyway. "Why don't you take her out on a date?" Seth suggested, since he had nothing else to contribute. "You've both been working so hard. Take her out, romance her a bit...get a bottle of wine...and you never know." It actually seemed like a pretty good idea. And he did have a goal to date Cynthia... Seth looked around at the restaurant he was sitting in, which was arguably the nicest place to eat in town in the amazing setting of the resort and got an idea of his own.

"It's not a bad idea." Trent nodded.

"No," Seth agreed. "It's not a bad idea at all."

Chapter Eight

IT HAD BEEN a long night of no sleep and an even longer day with no caffeine. Not only could she still not stomach coffee, she wasn't sure whether caffeine was safe for the baby and considering she couldn't get a doctor's appointment for a few more days, it seemed safer to abstain. At any rate, the combination of staying up most of the night fretting about her mother's response and no caffeine to kick-start her was not a good one. By the time she handed off the store to Colton at three, Cynthia was bagged and all she wanted to do was go home and lay on her couch.

After she tried to talk to her mother again, of course.

The night before, her mom had been more than a little upset with the news of Cynthia's pregnancy, and her reaction had been pretty far from what she'd expected. To be fair, she wasn't sure what she'd expected from her mom, but it wasn't anger and downright refusal to talk to her about it. No. She really hadn't expected that from her mom and to say it hadn't hurt would be a lie. It stung. Badly.

Her phone vibrated and she reluctantly looked at it. Another text from Kylie. Cynthia ignored it. Again. Kylie had been texting her all day, wanting to tell Cynthia about her new apartment in Vancouver and the campus and probably all kinds of other amazing things and Cynthia had been a crappy friend because all she could think of was how her life was imploding and coming to a screeching halt while her best friend's was just beginning.

It wasn't fair; she knew that. But she needed another day or two to process everything and try to sort things out with her mom before she told Kylie anything. Besides, Kylie and Malcolm would be back next weekend and she'd have a chance to tell her everything in person. Which would be so much better.

She was about to tuck her phone into her purse when it vibrated again. This time with a phone call. She answered it without thinking.

"I'm glad I caught you."

"Seth?" As a reflex, Cynthia looked up and down the street to see whether anyone she knew was there and could hear her conversation.

"Are you done working?"

"Yes. Why?"

"I'll pick you up in twenty minutes." It was a command, but there was a boyish charm in his voice, too. It was the only thing that kept her from hanging up.

"Pardon me? You'll do what?"

"You agreed to date me, remember?"

"I remember." She smiled a little but shook her head at the same time. "Have you ever been on a date before?"

"With you? No."

"No." She tried to keep the exasperation out of her voice. "Obviously not with me. I meant, with anyone. Because you don't just tell the girl you're going to pick her up in twenty minutes," she tried to explain. "You *ask* her. It's really quite simple." She tried to sound firm, but there was an unmistakable flutter of excitement in her belly at seeing Seth again. Shockingly, and against everything she could have dreamed of, he'd become the one positive in her life lately, and although she'd never admit it to him, the idea of seeing him instead of spending the evening with her mother and the tension between them sounded pretty damn good to her.

"Okay," Seth said through the phone. "I'll try again."

"Good. I think you—"

Cynthia looked at the cell phone in her hand. *Call Ended.* Maybe he'd gone through a dead spot; the mountains were notorious for spotty cell coverage. She was about to tuck her phone into her bag when it rang again. A smile tugged at the corners of her mouth when she saw it was Seth.

"Hi, Seth. Did you go through a—"

"Cynthia." He sounded very serious and formal. "I've called to ask you a very important question."

She almost burst out laughing when she realized what he'd done. He'd hung up on her to try again, just as he'd said he would. She did her best to sound serious when she asked, "And what is that?"

"By any chance are you free tonight?"

Her smile couldn't have been any broader and she nodded even though he couldn't see her. "As a matter of fact, I am."

"Would you do me the pleasure of accompanying me on a date this evening?"

She swallowed back a giggle. "That sounds lovely."

"I'll pick you up in twenty minutes." Seth quickly added, "If that's okay?"

"That's fine." She liked this cute and funny version of Seth. Almost as much as she liked the commanding, take-charge side of him. He never failed to surprise her. "I'll see you then."

Cynthia ended the call and before she could stop herself, she let out a squeal of joy. It was true that there were so many complications when it came to Seth, not the least of which was the fact that she was carrying his child. She may have agreed to the dating idea under duress—well, not really—but still, it was a forced decision. But none of that mattered, because at that moment, despite all the reasons not to be, she was excited.

"Well, well, Cynthia Giles." She spun around to see Suzy Crosswell next to her. She'd been so caught up in her phone conversation, Cynthia had forgotten she was in a public place.

"Hi Suzy. How are you?"

The other woman ignored the question and asked one of her own. "Who were you talking to just now? Because if I didn't know better, I would say that you are one smitten kitten."

Smitten kitten?

Cynthia blinked hard at Suzy before she finally shook her head. "Oh, I don't think so. That was just…" She searched her brain for a lie that would be believable. "That was Kylie. She was just telling me that she'd be back next weekend before she officially leaves."

From one look at Suzy, Cynthia knew the other woman didn't believe a word of her excuse, but to her credit she didn't call her out. Instead, she smiled and gave Cynthia a wink. "Whatever you say, dear. But I've seen a lot of women in love over the years, and you definitely have that glow."

She would have replied but before she could, the other woman disappeared down the sidewalk, humming as she went. It was probably a good thing, too, because Cynthia had no idea what she would have said.

FROM THE MOMENT Seth had come up with the idea of the date, he couldn't stop staring at his watch. He'd planned it perfectly to call her when she was done working. It actually surprised him a little that he knew her work schedule without even realizing it. He'd never before memorized any woman's work schedule. He would have put more meaning on that little detail, but he was too busy ironing out the rest of his plans.

Of course, the first step was getting her to agree to it, which he had, although not without a little hiccup. He smiled as he looked in the mirror. He hadn't expected her to give him any grief over the date, or more specifically, the way he asked. But he was glad she had. It wouldn't have been the same if Cynthia didn't put up a little fight. That was part of what made her so appealing. She didn't make it easy. And he liked it. He liked it a lot.

Declaring his reflection fit for an evening with a beautiful woman, he left the bathroom and grabbed the bouquet of flowers he'd picked up on his way home. Aware that he wasn't going to have too many shots at it, Seth was determined to make the most of every date Cynthia agreed to. She was carrying his child, and as if that wasn't enough reason to win her over, he knew it was more than that. Much more. Cynthia was different from any woman he'd ever met and he wasn't going to go down without a fight.

The drive to her house only took a minute. He picked his way up the snow-covered walkway, noting it didn't look as though it had been shoveled for quite some time. He knew she was busy with the store and of course her mom, but maybe she'd been busier than he knew. He spotted a shovel propped up against the gate; he got to work and quickly cleared the sidewalk of snow with the exception of a few stubborn spots of ice. He made a mental note to return and put some salt on them so Cynthia wouldn't slip. He retrieved the flowers from where he'd left them in the car and knocked on the door.

She opened it almost immediately, as if she'd been waiting. The sight of her made him take a step back so he could better take all of her in. She was breathtaking. He'd never seen her look anything less than fantastic, but somehow dressed in a simple green dress that was fitted at the waist before flaring out into a skirt that danced around her lean legs—legs he still fantasized having wrapped around him again—she literally took his breath away. The vision of her affected the part of his brain that allowed him to formulate words.

"Hi." Her brows knitted together in concern and Seth took a deep breath, giving him enough oxygen to function.

"You look amazing, Cynthia."

She blushed a little then. Only enough to color her cheeks, but it was sexy as hell. "You look pretty good yourself." She took her time as she looked him up and down. "Who knew you cleaned up so well?"

"There's a lot you don't know about me."

She laughed. "I'm not sure about that. Are those for me?" She gestured with her head toward the bouquet he clutched.

"Actually, no." The smile fell from her face and he quickly added, "They're for your mother."

"My mother?" She blinked fast, and he hoped she wouldn't cry. He hadn't meant it as anything more than a kind gesture to brighten up her room on a winter's day.

"I just thought…"

"Thank you." She took the flowers and disappeared into the house for a moment. When she returned, she no longer looked as if she was going to cry. "I'll take them to her later," she said. "It'll just be a lot of explaining if I do it now and… well, it's complicated." Her beautiful face clouded over. There was definitely something she wasn't saying and as much as Seth wanted to know what it was, it wasn't the time for it. Not yet.

She reached for her coat, which he deftly took from her and held out so she could shrug into it. She fastened each button until he could no longer see the delicious swell of her breasts bursting out of the top of her dress. Breasts he'd love to have his hands on again. To kiss, and tease and—*no*. This date was not about getting her into bed. As much as he'd love to do that. Tonight was all about showing her what kind of guy he could be—that he was. It was about showing her that he wanted to really try this thing with her. Because as much as it continued to surprise him, he was pretty sure that was exactly what he wanted to do.

He held his arm out for her. "Shall we?"

Seth half-expected her to argue or make a smart aleck comment; instead, she smiled and threaded her arm through his. He led her down the shoveled walk and into the truck.

"Thank you," she said when they drove away.

"For what?"

"For shoveling. I just haven't had a chance."

"No problem. It was—"

"And the flowers," she interrupted him. "That was really sweet. I didn't really expect—"

"You didn't expect me to be sweet?"

She smiled and shook her head. "Honestly? No. But you're surprising me a lot these days."

Seth swallowed his grin. "The surprises aren't over yet."

Chapter Nine

SETH HADN'T BEEN LYING when he said the surprises were just beginning. They pulled up to the Springs and Cynthia knew right away they were going to be eating at the Stillwater. Except when he led them into the hotel, instead of turning down the corridor to the Stillwater, he turned the other way.

"Are we going to eat? Because you know, a hungry pregnant woman is not a pretty sight."

He smiled down at her. "I don't know—I think this hungry pregnant woman is a very pretty sight." He tucked a piece of hair behind her ear in a move that was very intimate and one Cynthia would normally pull away from. But things were different between them now in a way she couldn't quite put her finger on. "And yes," he continued. "We're going to eat."

"But the restaurant is the other way." She half spun to point in the opposite direction, but he gently spun her around and continued to walk away from the Stillwater.

"I know exactly where it is," Seth said with a devilish grin. "Who said we were going to be eating in the restaurant?"

She shut up then and kept walking with him. She hadn't spent a great deal of time in the Springs, mostly because she'd been too busy to join the girls when they'd done *ladies' days* at the spa. But she knew where the pools were, because she—like almost everyone who'd ever seen it—could never forget it. The corridor opened up on a floor-to-ceiling vaulted wall of glass that enclosed the pools. Inside there was a variety of pools, both large for all hotel guests, and small private ones.

Seth led her up to the glass wall, and then over to the sliding doors that opened into the pools. Together they walked past the attendants at the desk who'd clearly been expecting them, with a nod and smile. She looked around and took everything in. People lounged in the healing hot spring water, or swam laps in the cooler pool—those were the main pools. Little paths branched off the main walkway, which Cynthia assumed led to the private pools, but they were secluded with trees, boulders, and plants, so she couldn't see beyond the entrances.

"This is us." Seth's voice broke her out of her private thoughts and she looked to see that they'd stopped in front of one of those private pathways.

"We're going swimming?"

He laughed. "Come on."

The path was narrow so he gestured for her to walk ahead of him, which she did. It didn't take her long to make her way along the stones and into the opening. When she did, she stopped short and put her hand to her mouth. "Oh." Tears sprung to her eyes and she turned around to see Seth behind her with a single white rose in his hand. "You did all this?"

"For you."

She took the rose and turned around again to take it all in.

They were indeed at a private pool, with a bubbling water-fall tucked at one end. Candles of all shapes and sizes lit up the space and reflected off the water, where white rose petals floated and danced in the gentle currents of the pool. A table was set up with more rose petals on the blue tablecloth and two plates were covered by silver domes.

"It's beautiful, Seth." It was more than that, but she couldn't seem to find the words to describe it properly. He came up behind her and wrapped his arms around her waist in a way that was both so familiar, and so foreign, it momentarily shocked her. "Thank you," she breathed. "No one has ever done anything like this for me before."

He nuzzled his head into her neck, but didn't kiss her. His proximity sent a thrill through her, right to her core. "I'm glad I could be the one to give it to you. You deserve all of this, and so much more. I told you I was going to surprise you."

She nodded but couldn't find words.

"We should eat." He moved away from her so abruptly she felt his absence keenly. "After all, wasn't it you who said something about a hungry pregnant woman?"

Cynthia laughed and sat in the chair he pulled out for her.

For the next hour they ate, laughed, and talked. It was the first time Cynthia could remember actually talking to Seth without arguing or flirting. It was nice. Really nice. And he was right: he was full of surprises. She never would have guessed him to be so passionate about the ski hill and all his ideas to expand the business. She'd never figured him for a motivated and driven man who seemed to want more out of life than one constant party. Not for the first time, she considered the very real possibility that she'd misjudged him.

When the conversation shifted to Cynthia's mother, she tensed the way she always did, but then instead of stopping herself, she opened up. "I told her about the baby."

"Good." Seth straightened up in his chair. "What did she say? Was she excited?"

"Not exactly." Cynthia shook her head and twisted the napkin in her hand. "She kind of closed off and got mad at me for telling her. I don't know what to think."

Seth's face lined with concern and he reached out for her hand. "It's probably just a shock," he said. "I mean, it was a shock for us, too, right? And it's not like we were dating or anything. I mean, as far as your mom knows, you weren't even seeing anyone."

She opened her mouth to say, *I'm still not seeing anyone.* But somehow that didn't feel as truthful anymore. Instead, she nodded. "You're probably right. Tonight, when I take her the flowers that you brought, I'll talk to her again. It'll be okay."

He squeezed her hand in his and she looked up into Seth's eyes. "It *will* be okay, Cynthia. All of it. I can't fix things for your mom and for that I'm so sorry." She nodded and willed herself not to cry. "But when it comes to us," he continued, "you, me and the baby—that I can do something about. And I know we're going into this totally backward, but I meant it when I said I liked you. A lot. This is just the beginning."

"Seth, you don't have to—"

"I know I don't. I want to. But right now, I really want to go for a dip in that pool. What do you think?"

She laughed at the sudden change of topic. "I don't know. Is it safe? I mean, for the…" She put her hand on her stomach.

"It is." Seth let go of her hand and stood. "I checked with the powers that be and the temperature in this pool is safe for pregnant women."

"But I don't have a suit."

He raised an eyebrow and she felt a hot blush creep over her body.

"Seth, I'm not—"

"Calm down. I took care of it." He pointed to a small wooden table stacked with white plush towels and what looked like a bikini and a pair of shorts. "Behind that tree, there's a little private change room. I'll wait here."

The water did look inviting, and he had taken care of all

the details. Besides, Cynthia wasn't ready to let the evening end. With a shrug and a smile, she went to change.

EVERYTHING HAD GONE off without a hitch in his master first date plan. Seth had called in a lot of favors from Trent, and of course Carmen had helped with the details, and Jax had provided the amazing meal. He owed them all big time, but it was worth it to see Cynthia's reaction and to see her open up to him. The more time he spent with her, the more he wanted to be with her. And to his surprise, it had nothing to do with the fact that she was carrying his child except that it only made her more beautiful to him. The more time that passed, the more certain Seth was that he was falling for her.

By the time he changed, Cynthia was already in the water, her head tipped back, her eyes closed and a look of sheer relaxation on her features. He slipped into the water across from her and let the heat envelope him. "It's nice, isn't it?"

"Perfect," she mumbled without opening her eyes. "I can't believe I've never done this before."

"What? A hot tub?"

She nodded but still didn't open her eyes.

He settled into the small pool so he sat just across from her. He had to continually remind himself that they were on a first date, and despite the fact that they'd done everything in their relationship up until that point completely backward, he was going to make sure he acted like a complete gentleman all night. As much as he wanted to, and man did he want to, he was not going to do anything inappropriate. It was safer to sit across from her, out of arm's reach. She lifted her head and sat up, exposing her bikini-clad breasts. His body responded hard and fast. Yes, it was much safer on the opposite side of the pool.

"I'm glad you're enjoying it," Seth said after a moment.

Finally, she opened her eyes and smiled. "I am. So much. Thank you again for all of this. It really wasn't necessary."

"Yes, it was." He stretched his arms out along the edge of the pool and he didn't miss the flash of desire in Cynthia's eyes as she noticed his exposed chest. *Good*, he thought. At least the attraction was mutual. Not that he needed any further confirmation on that particular aspect. That had never been their problem. "I told you I was going to prove to you that I was more than you think I am."

She tipped her head and her lips pressed together. "Seth, I shouldn't have said any of that stuff about you being a player and not the relationship type. It wasn't right of me to say it."

"Yes it was," he said simply. "You were exactly right. There wasn't anything you said that wasn't true. There's a reason I have that reputation." He did a quick mental scan of his last few years. No doubt he'd earned his reputation. But what Cynthia hadn't factored into the equation was one very important detail. "There's one thing you didn't consider, though."

"What's that?"

"The only reason I've never been the type to settle down was because I'd never met anyone worth settling down for." The smile fell off her face and she shook her head. "What?"

"I want to believe that."

"Then believe it." Instinctively he wanted to reach for her, but he held himself back. "It's the truth, Cynthia. Before you, there was never anyone worth settling down for."

She shook her head again but didn't speak.

"What are you thinking?" She wouldn't look at him, so he pressed. "Cynthia, talk to me. This isn't going to work if we can't be honest with each other. I need you to—"

"You didn't want anything to do with me until you found out I was pregnant."

Seth sat up with a splash. "What?"

101

"It's true. I was just another conquest to you," she continued, speaking so rapidly it was hard to keep up. "You didn't want anything to do with me after we hooked up. You barely even spoke to me afterwards and then there was the woman at the restaurant."

"What woman?"

"At the Stillwater, after we were together. I saw you having dinner together and—"

"Cassidy Langly?" He almost laughed. "She's the business manager for Stone Summit. We were having a meeting about the Slush Cup." He searched her eyes for some indication that she believed him. "I was pitching the idea to her. I needed her on board before going to Malcolm with it."

"It was a business meeting?"

"Yes." He smiled. "Don't tell me you were jealous?" The fact that she'd been jealous gave him a little thrill, but it also pissed him off. Had that simple meeting been the cause for all the mistrust between them?

"I wasn't." She stuck out her chin in defiance. "It was just…it was just disappointing because I thought we maybe had something and then I saw that and…" She looked down and her words drifted off.

"We do have something." He waited until she looked at him before he continued. "We've had something from the very start and it's so much more than—what?" She'd started to shake her head again, and wouldn't look at him. "Cynthia?"

"It's just…it wasn't until you found out that I was pregnant that you wanted to date me or whatever it is that we're doing here and it's only so you can be part of the baby's life. Well, don't worry. You can be. I'm not that type of person. I'd never keep you apart from your child." She stood and turned, headed for the steps of the pool. Water dripped off all the perfect curves of her body, but for the first time, Seth hardly noticed her fine form, he was so focused on what she was telling him. "You don't have to worry," she kept talking, her back to him. "And you can relax with this big show that you're a good guy. It's not necessary. I believe you, and I—"

Before she could take another step away from him, Seth wrapped one arm around her waist and spun her hard and fast into his chest, where he caught and held her tight. Her mouth was open in surprise, and he crushed his lips to hers. She needed to stop trying to convince herself there was nothing between them, when as far as he was concerned, there was everything between them. And certainly, having a baby was an addition he hadn't factored on, but it was far from the reason he held her in his arms, kissing her as if everything in the world depended on it.

It took her a few seconds to become aware of what was going on, and when she did, Seth felt her body relax and she kissed him back with all the heat he was giving her. The chemistry between them was undeniable; it always had been. She needed to remember that.

When the kiss was finally over, and Seth was convinced he'd made his point, he gently pulled away, but didn't release his grip on her. "You need to stop talking, woman, and listen."

Her chest heaved against his in a maddening way that was trying every last shred of willpower he had left.

"I'm listening," she breathed.

"I'm only going to say this one time." His voice was low, but hard as he stared into her eyes and forced her to focus on him. "This has nothing to do with the baby." She opened her mouth, but he placed a finger on her lips, and she closed it again. "This has everything to do with me and you. From the first time I kissed you, I knew there was something between us. Something real. Running into you again in the Paw that night? That wasn't a coincidence, Cynthia. I sought you out. Nothing about our time together has been a mistake or a coincidence. The fact that you're pregnant with my child...yes. Maybe that wasn't planned, but it in no way changes how I feel about you. If you only hear one thing I'm saying, hear this. The baby isn't the reason I'm trying to convince you I'm a good guy with actual feelings for you. *You* are the reason. I've never met anyone worth settling down for. Until you. You are every reason, Cynthia. Just you."

Tears filled her eyes, but she didn't look away. "But…the baby?"

One hand slid down her body to rest on her stomach and the life within. "I'd be lying if I told you I wasn't scared. I'm terrified. But not because of anything to do with us. I have a million fears about being a good father and knowing how to change a diaper and support the head, or whatever else I'm supposed to do or not do." She smiled then, and Seth felt his heart swell a little. "But I'm not scared of you, or more specifically how I feel about you. I'm absolutely falling for you, Cynthia Giles. My biggest fear is that I can't convince you to fall along with me."

The tears spilled from her eyes and into the water below. She raised her head to his and kissed him slow and sweet before she pulled back again. "You know, for a guy who says he isn't good with words, you did pretty damn good."

HER MIND REELED from everything Seth had just said. There were a million reasons not to believe what he was saying. A million reasons she should walk away and not get any further involved with him than she already was. It was totally possible to raise a child without being together. Lots of couples did it and did it well.

Logically, she knew a lot of things. But as she pulled away from Seth's arms and retreated to the other side of the pool where she could clear her head, Cynthia knew it wasn't about logic.

Maybe being in love with Seth McBride was not a requirement for having this baby. But it wouldn't hurt. And if she was honest with herself, she'd been falling a little more in love with him every day. It was all happening quickly. Too quickly. But she didn't have the luxury of time and if Seth and everything he'd just said to her was to be believed, she didn't need it.

"Tell me what you're thinking."

She shook her head and laughed. "So many things." With one wet hand, she smoothed back the stray hairs that had come loose from the bun on the back of her head. "I think you're crazy and everything you're saying to me is totally insane." She waited for that to sink in before she continued. "But I also kind of believe you."

"Kind of?"

She nodded, suddenly shy. "Okay, more than kind of. I can't explain it…"

"You don't have to."

"You're right, I don't." She smiled. "Because everything about this is crazy, but I don't care. I like you."

"You like me?"

She nodded. She wasn't ready to say anymore. Part of her, a large part of her, wanted to throw it all out there and lay it all out the way Seth had, but she couldn't. It was too much. Her hands went to her still flat stomach. She knew it wouldn't be that way for long. There were about to be a lot of changes in her life; most of them she had very little control over. But she did have control over this one little thing. It seemed like such a small thing, but at least for the moment, she needed to hold on to it.

"That's all I'm ready for right now, okay?"

He walked toward her with the sexiest smile on his face; every nerve ending in her body came alive. "That's more than okay." He bent down, put his hands on her hips and lifted her out of the water to set her on the edge of the pool as if she weighed nothing. His lips met hers in a soft, sensual kiss that had her body arching into him. "I can work with this," he said, his voice deep and low in his throat. "I can definitely work with this."

Oh yes, Cynthia thought as she pulled him in for another kiss. If being with Seth meant feeling like an internal fire had been lit every time he touched her, she could definitely work with their situation as well. When he moved his lips down her neck, to the swell of her breasts, she heard a low groan that she only vaguely recognized as coming from her. His mouth was like molten lava working its way down her body, and for a moment, she thought she might explode from only his kiss. But then before he moved lower, to the thin line where her bikini met her stomach, he pressed a kiss to her belly and whispered, "I love you already."

It took her half a beat to realize he wasn't talking to her at all and she had to bite her lip to keep her emotions in check. The moment was so powerful, all thoughts of having him inside her vanished.

"Seth?" Her voice was soft, but she knew he heard her. "I have a doctor appointment on Monday. Why don't you come?"

He stood and kissed her gently on the mouth. "I wouldn't miss it for anything."

Chapter Ten

"YOU CAN LOOK AT ME, you know?"

"I know." Seth kept his eyes firmly locked on the corkboard in the doctor's office and the variety of notices they had pinned there. "I'm reading."

Cynthia laughed. "Really? And what are you finding out?"

"Well, if you must know, there are all kinds of interesting things here. For example…" Seth scanned the board. "They're looking for people with asthma to conduct a new study."

"Interesting." He could hear the laughter in her voice. "What else is so riveting you can't turn and look at me?"

He shook his head and read the first notice his eyes landed on. "Cracked nipples? Engorged—oh good God." Horrified, he turned away quickly and Cynthia only laughed harder.

"I think that's a breastfeeding support group," she said between chuckles.

"You need support for that?"

She nodded. "So I've heard."

"And your nipples, they…" He shuddered, not wanting to think about it.

Cynthia held out her hand and with a deep sense of relief,

Seth went to her side and took it in his own. Seth couldn't remember the last time he'd been in a doctor's office, and he'd sure as hell never been there with a woman who was covered only in a thin cotton sheet that wasn't leaving much to the imagination. Not that he was turned on—okay, not really. Mostly he was freaking out.

"Stop freaking out," she said, reading his mind.

"I'm not—okay, I am."

"Why? This is just a routine appointment." Cynthia squeezed his hand. "I've known Dr. Gordon my whole life. Besides, he's not going to tell us anything we don't already know. I'm pregnant."

"I know." Seth took a deep breath. How could he explain that doctors made him nervous? And don't even get him started on hospitals. The smell, the sounds, the fluorescent lights that made everything a watery shade of yellow: there was nothing good about a hospital. People went there to die. He'd only been a boy when his mother went in for a routine gall-bladder surgery and—

After a knock on the door, it opened to reveal a very attractive, very young woman who could not possibly be a doctor, despite the white coat she wore.

Cynthia dropped his hand and let out a short squeal before the doctor-girl ran forward and wrapped Cynthia into a tight hug. Seth looked between the two women, his anxiety momentarily forgotten in the wake of the totally unexpected greeting of the doctor who was supposed to be a man.

He waited as long as was decent, longer really, before he cleared his throat. "And you are?"

Cynthia laughed and they broke apart. "I'm so sorry. Seth, this is Deanna. We went to school together." She looked vaguely familiar, but despite the fact that they'd apparently all gone to the same school, there were a few years between them and he couldn't quite place her. Cynthia turned to the woman again. "Deanna? What are you doing here?"

"I'm so sorry." Deanna straightened her white coat. Her doctor's coat. "That was so unprofessional of me." She turned to Seth and stuck out her hand. "Hi, I'm Dr. Gordon. I don't think we really knew each other in high school."

He shook her hand. "No, I don't think we did. It's nice to meet you. I guess we're waiting for your...dad?"

"The nurse didn't clear it with you?" Deanna turned back to Cynthia.

"Clear what?"

"I'll be temporarily taking over some of my dad's patient load," Deanna explained. "She's supposed to check with everyone when they come in to make sure it's okay. I'm so sorry. I just assumed...if it's too weird for you, Cynthia, I can go get—"

"No." Cynthia laughed. "It's totally fine. I'm just so happy you're back in town. It's been so long."

"Well, medical degrees don't come quickly." Deanna smiled and Seth relaxed a little bit. If Cynthia was fine with the arrangement, he was too. Besides, she did seem like a nice person, and obviously Cynthia liked her. That could only be a good thing. "But I'm only here temporarily," Deanna added. "Just until Dad can find someone more permanent to help him out."

"You don't want to stay in Cedar Springs?" Seth asked.

It was Cynthia who answered. "Ever since we were little girls, Deanna's been planning on how to get out of town. She's always had big dreams."

"It's true." Deanna smiled. "And I still do. Like I said, this is temporary. Ever since Dad's last birthday, he's decided he wants to scale back and spend more time with Mom. Not that I blame him or anything, but I'm not going to be his solution."

"What's wrong with Cedar Springs?" Seth asked. "It's not

so bad." He squeezed Cynthia's hand and she turned to smile at him.

"It's fine." Deanna turned her attention to Cynthia's chart. "It's just not for me." She scanned the pages before she closed it again. "Enough about me. Let's talk about you." She put a smile on her face and looked back to Cynthia and then over to Seth. "We took a little blood when you came in…" Cynthia bit her bottom lip and nodded to Deanna's unasked question.

"Right," Deanna said. "But I'm sure you already know that the test came back positive."

Cynthia nodded again. "But I'm not really sure…I mean, we're not really sure…how long it's been."

Deanna smiled broadly in response. "Then I think it's time we find out, don't you?"

It was Seth who said yes with more enthusiasm then even he'd expected. He stepped forward and took Cynthia's hand again when Deanna added, "Why don't you lay back and we'll get started?"

DEANNA, or Dr. Gordon as she should probably call her, squirted the jelly onto Cynthia's exposed stomach and picked up the Doppler wand.

"What's that?"

Cynthia bit back the urge to giggle again. Seth had been a mass of nerves from the moment they'd walked into the clinic. The paradox between the big strong man and the jittery mess he'd become would have been even funnier if Cynthia didn't know a little bit about where it stemmed from. She didn't know many of the details of Seth's mother's passing, but she did know he'd been young, and clearly the circumstances had affected him. She wouldn't have teased him at about it at all except the teasing seemed to relax him.

"This is the Doppler wand. All it does is give us a view inside so we can see the baby."

"We're going to see the baby?" A smile slid over Seth's features and Deanna nodded.

"Yes." She handled Seth's questions with ease. "But it probably won't look like much yet—it's pretty early—so don't be alarmed if you have trouble making out the details."

"But that's normal, right?"

"Perfectly."

"So, we'll be able to—"

"Seth." Cynthia put her hand over his and squeezed. "Let Dr. Gordon do her job. It will be okay, I promise." He looked down at her with so much trust, Cynthia felt a little tug on her heart. To see this big, strong, totally in charge man so unsure was...touching. Even more so because he so clearly trusted her. She took a deep breath, suddenly overwhelmed by what that might mean.

"Are you ready, Cynthia?"

She nodded and Deanna placed the Doppler wand on her belly and moved it slowly. All three of them stared at the screen, but as far as Cynthia could tell, if there was anything there, it looked like a bunch of smudges and smears. She couldn't make out a thing. The way that Seth stared so intensely, she wouldn't be surprised if he could see something. But she had no idea how.

Deanna moved the wand around and clicked buttons on her screen for a few minutes. Cynthia finally gave up trying to see anything and stared at the ceiling. Then she heard it. It was muffled and sounded as though she had her ear to a fishbowl and was listening underwater, but Cynthia definitely heard it.

Seth spoke. "That's the...that's..."

"The heartbeat." Deanna smiled. "I wasn't sure we'd be able to hear it today, but there it is."

They were all silent for a few minutes. Cynthia closed her

eyes and absorbed the sound of her baby's heartbeat beating inside her. Her own heart swelled when Seth slipped his hand to her shoulder and squeezed. In that one moment, for better or worse, their strange, ill-conceived family felt absolutely perfect.

All too soon, Deanna switched off the speaker and Cynthia felt her stomach being wiped clean. Her gown was pulled back into place, and Cynthia propped herself up on her elbows to look at the doctor. "So?"

"From what I can tell with the dates you gave me and the baby's measurements, I'd figure you're about ten weeks along now."

"Ten?" Cynthia tried to do the math in her head. "That means—"

"You're almost through your first trimester."

Cynthia nodded.

"Okay, I'll let you get dressed. Why don't you make an appointment for about a month from now? But in the meantime, I'd love to grab a tea and catch up."

The women made plans to see each other soon and Seth followed the doctor out while she got changed. A few minutes later, she joined Seth—who looked markedly more relaxed—in the lobby and after she made a follow-up appointment, was finally ready to go when Deanna's father, the elder Dr. Gordon, caught up with her.

"Cynthia. I'm glad I saw you before you could sneak out of here."

He always had a warm smile on his face, the same smile Cynthia remembered while he put a plaster cast on her arm when she was eight and told her everything would be okay. The same smile that had been present at all of her mother's appointments after the hospital released her into his palliative care. There was something about the man that was reassuring, even when Cynthia knew there couldn't possibly be a positive outcome as far as Mom was concerned. She gave him a quick hug. "It's good to see you, Dr. Gordon, but a nice surprise seeing Deanna here, too."

"It's been nice having her help out her old man, that's for sure. Now we just need to convince her and all her youthful energy to take over the practice." Dr. Gordon crossed his arms over his chest, and his smile dimmed slightly. "I missed you at your mother's appointment last week."

Last week? Her mother didn't have an appointment last week. "Yes, well…"

"She said you were very busy with the store," Dr. Gordon said quickly, but she didn't miss the look in his eyes. He knew she had no idea her mother had been in. No doubt Jess had taken her, but why wouldn't she tell Cynthia? "But I'm sure she filled you in on her latest test results."

Cynthia blinked hard. There was no point lying. "No." She shook her head. "How are they?"

Dr. Gordon shook his head, but the kind smile was back, this time tinged with sadness. "You know I'm not at liberty to discuss a patient's test results, Cynthia." She did know that. She also knew there was a reason he'd brought it up.

"Dr. Gordon, you know I—"

He took her hands in his and stared into her eyes. "Talk to your mom, Cynthia." She nodded; understanding filled her. "Soon."

SETH WAS NEEDED BACK at Stone Summit. Although he wouldn't miss the baby's first doctor appointment for anything, it was incredibly hard to take time off with Malcolm out of town. He'd put the business manager, Cassidy Langly, in touch with Marcus to organize the party he seemed determined to throw, so at least that was off his plate. But he still had the details for the Slush Cup to arrange and his phone had buzzed in his pocket the entire time they'd been in the clinic.

He'd planned to walk Cynthia to the store, and then take off, but one look at her face after Dr. Gordon mentioned her mother and he knew that there was nothing as important as being with Cynthia at that moment.

"Come on." He took her hand and gently led her out onto Main Street. "Let me buy you a tea and one of Suzy's cinnamon buns."

She didn't object, only nodded slightly and let him lead her down the street to Dream Puffs. The moment they walked through the door and the bell chimed, the warm sweetness of the bakery enveloped them like a hug. He left Cynthia in a booth tucked into the corner with as much privacy as they could manage, and went to place their order.

Suzy Crosswell's eyes were bright with questions, but to her credit, she was perceptive enough to know whatever questions she wanted to ask about the two of them together, they would have to wait. Seth returned to the table with their order and sat across from her.

"Your mother," he said after a moment. "What day did you tell her about the baby?"

"Last Thursday."

"And she saw Dr. Gordon…"

"Last Thursday." He saw the exact moment it all made sense to Cynthia and she looked up; her eyes swam with tears. "That must have been why she reacted the way she did." She blinked slowly. A fat teardrop fell to the table. "Seth, she's really sick."

He covered her hand with his own.

"She's going to die."

"I know, babe." His voice was low and his heart broke for her. "I know."

The pain on her face was so sharp and strong, he ached

knowing he couldn't take it away for her. She lowered her head and sobs overtook her. Seth didn't say a word. He just held her hands, giving her the strength she needed to draw upon. Their drinks grew cold and finally, Cynthia's tears dried up. "I need to go."

He nodded. "I'll walk you home."

"What about the store?"

"I'll take care of it."

"But, I—"

"I've got it." He pulled her gently out of the booth and wrapped his arm around her, tucking her up against his shoulder for support.

They were just walking out the door when Suzy stopped him and handed him a paper bag. "I thought Linda might like a cinnamon bun. They were always her favorite."

Cynthia managed a small smile and Seth nodded his thanks.

He let Cynthia lean on him and he supported her light weight for the short walk to her house. She needed to conserve all the strength she had—physical, and especially mental, for the days that lay ahead.

"I'll come by later, okay?"

She shook her head. "You don't have to."

"I'll bring dinner." He ignored her protests. "Don't worry about anything, okay? Just be with your mom."

She didn't argue. He kissed her lightly on the lips and before she went inside, he pressed a photo into her hand. "Deanna gave me this while you were getting changed."

Cynthia looked down at the ultrasound photo and a smile tugged at her lips.

"Now go show your mom her grandchild."

Chapter Eleven

CYNTHIA WAS careful to keep her face neutral when she walked into the kitchen. She was certainly upset, but not with Jess and after everything the other woman had done for them, she didn't want her to think she was anything other than grateful.

"I ran into Dr. Gordon at the clinic today," Cynthia said. "The older Dr. Gordon." That was an important clarification and as it turned out, it was all that was needed for Jess to put the pieces together.

"Cynthia, I'm sorry." Jess held her hand up. "I was only doing what she asked and I don't know why she didn't want to tell you. I didn't think it was right, but you know your mother and how she can be and it wasn't really my place and—"

"It's okay. I'm not mad, Jess." Cynthia handed her the paper bag from Dream Puffs. "I know exactly how she can be. And I don't know all the details. I'll ask her. But Dr. Gordon did mention the appointment I didn't even know she had."

Jess put the cinnamon buns on a plate while she spoke. "She didn't want to worry you. I know it doesn't make sense, but she is your mother and she's worried about how hard you work. You've had so much going on with the store and trying to do it all on your own. And that was even before the..." She turned with the plate and tears flooded her eyes. It couldn't be easy to spend day after day with someone when your sole job was to make them comfortable so they could die at home.

Impulsively, Cynthia pulled Jess into a hug. "Thank you," she said. "You've been so great being here and helping. I know this hasn't been easy for you either."

Jess pulled away and wiped at her eyes. "No. Don't thank me for anything," she said between sniffs. "I knew what I was getting into when I signed up. I love Linda, but it's not me I'm worried about, Cynthia. With everything you have to deal with and now the baby..." She shook her head and grabbed a tissue. "I didn't even ask you how your appointment was. Did it go okay?"

"It was great." Cynthia smiled as she remembered Seth's reaction to the ultrasound. "I'm almost three months along and..." Cynthia handed Jess the ultrasound photo. "I have the baby's first picture."

Jess took it and immediately put her hand to her mouth. "Oh my goodness. It's so...wow, the baby is..." She burst into laughter. "I can't make out a thing."

Cynthia laughed along with her because no matter how hard she stared at it, she couldn't see anything more than a blob which she assumed was the baby, and a dark spot that Deanna had pointed out on the screen as the heart. "I know." She took the picture back. "I don't see it either. But I'm kind of hoping Mom might..." She trailed off as she realized that she wasn't really sure at all what she hoped from her mom. To talk about the baby? Certainly. To accept her child? Absolutely. But beyond that, she had no idea what her mother was thinking and evidently, they were running short on time.

"She's going to love it, Cynthia." Jess smiled kindly. "Go and talk to her." She held out the tray of cinnamon buns and tea she'd added to the tray. Cynthia propped up the ultrasound picture against a teacup and took the tray.

She took a deep breath and walked down the hall.

Her mother's door was open and Cynthia slipped inside, not wanting to disturb her if she was sleeping. She wasn't. Propped up in a nest of pillows, her once strong, vibrant mother looked even more frail than the last time they'd spoken. Cynthia didn't realize it was possible for one to deteriorate so fast. But her mother seemed to be wasting away a little more every day, if it was even possible.

"Hi, Mom." She put the tray on the table and sat on the bed, picking up her mom's hand. "How are you feeling today?"

"I'm glad you're here." Cynthia noticed she didn't answer her question, but she wasn't going to say anything. There was no good answer to that question. "I missed you."

She tried not to let guilt creep in and cloud her thinking. It was true that Cynthia's visits had been sparse since their first and totally failed conversation about the baby the week before. She should probably feel badly about that, but she'd needed the space to get everything straight in her head. After her date with Seth, she'd brought in the flowers, but her mother had been sleeping, so they couldn't talk. And truthfully, she'd shied away from any further conversation. But that was about to change.

"I've missed you, too, Mom. So much. But I needed to——"

"I know." Linda squeezed her eyes shut for a second. When she opened them again, they were shiny with tears. "I'm so sorry about the way I reacted when you told me…it's just…"

Cynthia nodded and took over. "Dr. Gordon told me you'd been to see him. It was the same day I told you about the baby."

"It was."

"What did he tell you?"

When she didn't answer right away, Cynthia pushed. "How long?"

Linda managed a watery smile.

"Mom."

"There are more masses…everywhere. There's nothing…"

"Mom? How long?"

"Any day."

Her voice was barely a whisper, but the words reverberated in her head and something inside her felt torn in half. She wanted to crumple into a heap and cry until there were no more tears. She wanted to scream and cry and break something at the injustice of losing her mother just as she was becoming one herself. She wanted to do all of those things; instead, she swallowed down the sob that threatened to escape. She slowly raised her mother's fragile hand and pressed her lips to the thin skin, breathing in deeply.

She held her there for a moment, just long enough to be sure she wouldn't break when she spoke. When she felt ready, Cynthia looked into her mother's eyes, a reflection of her own, only slightly dimmed from the cancer that ravaged her body. She moved her mother's hand and pressed it to her stomach where her grandchild grew, oblivious of the beautiful woman she or he would never get the chance to meet. "Say hi," she whispered with a small smile.

A single tear slipped down her mother's cheek and she matched Cynthia's smile. "Hello, my beautiful grandbaby." She spoke to the baby, but held Cynthia's eyes. "You're a pretty lucky baby," she continued. "You have a gorgeous mama with so much love and I promise I'll be your guardian angel, sweet thing. I'll be right there with you, every day."

It was then that Cynthia let herself cry. The tears rolled down her face unchecked as she climbed up into bed next to her mother, careful not to bump or jostle her. She nestled her head on her mother's pillow just like when she was a child and, starting at the beginning, Cynthia told her all about Seth, the baby, and how maybe, just maybe, she might be falling for him.

SETH SAID he'd handle things. And he did. But it wasn't easy. After leaving Cynthia at her house, he went straight over to the Store Room and told Colton everything that was happening. Thankfully, Cynthia hired well, and Colton was a good kid who was willing to help out as much as possible with whatever he could so Cynthia could spend time with her mom. But he was still in school and even though he wanted to, Seth in good conscience could not ask him to skip class. After a few phone calls, he'd managed to secure Kari Fox, who worked up at the Springs. Seth didn't know her well, but as soon as she explained the situation, Kari told him not to worry about the day shifts. It didn't occur to him until after that she would likely have had to use vacation time at the Springs in order to cover for things at the store, but Seth made a note to talk to Trent and Dylan about it.

It was late afternoon by the time he pulled his truck into the parking lot at Stone Summit, and he still had a whole days' worth of work ahead of him. The euphoria from seeing the ultrasound had all but been forgotten. That was, until he got a text message from Cynthia with a photo of the picture he'd given her for Linda. He smiled and made the picture his background screen before he texted her back.

Is everything going ok?

He walked into the shed, eager to check on the puppies before he locked himself in the office. His phone buzzed with Cynthia's response right as Nala and her three pups heard him enter. With one loud welcoming bark, and a series of puppy yips, they rushed to greet him.

Sad. But good.

Seth turned his phone around on the puppies, who scampered all over his feet trying to get to him, and snapped a picture to send her. That would make her smile. At least for a moment, and that's how he'd handle it. Moment by moment.

"Hey, Nala." He rubbed the dog's head and stood. "What do you say to a little fresh air?" The puppies were getting bigger every day and soon they'd need homes. Of course, he'd promised Cynthia that Nala could live with her. The thought made him smile. The comfort of the dog might be exactly what Cynthia needed.

Cynthia texted back a simple smiley face and Seth tucked his phone away while he watched the little balls of fluff roll and play in the snow as their mother stood guard.

"It's about time you showed up around here." Marcus appeared around the corner. "I was beginning to think you'd bailed on us."

"*Us?*"

"Malcolm and—"

"You?" Seth shook his head. He shouldn't be surprised that Marcus had slid back into things so easily. He'd always been very smooth at getting what he wanted. "I guess I didn't realize you were back for good."

"I told you the other day I thought Malcolm needed help around here."

Seth bent down and picked up a pup that chewed on his boot. "You say a lot of things, Marcus. I didn't realize you really wanted to stay."

Marcus nodded. "Fair. But I do. And I am. It's time I settled down."

Seth laughed out loud, which startled the puppy. "Now I know something must be wrong. You? Settle down?" But even as he laughed, he realized it wasn't all that long ago the idea of him settling down would have been laughable as well. Now it was all he could think about. He swallowed hard. "Seriously, what about the pro circuit? Why would you want to give that up for small-town life?"

Marcus shrugged and bent to pat one of the dogs so Seth couldn't see his face. "Felt like a change is all."

"From snowboarding?" There was more to the story, that was for sure, but Seth knew he wouldn't be able to get it out of him. Nor was it any of his business. Besides, Marcus had a point; they could use a little help around the hill. Especially if he planned to be there for Cynthia. And he did. "Whatever," he added. "Your life, I guess."

"It is. So you think Malcolm will hire me?" He stood again and ran a hand through his hair.

"You haven't asked him? I just assumed you'd cleared this with your brother."

"Well, after the opening and everything with Kylie..." Marcus kicked at the snow. "Well, I was thinking it would be better to maybe ease him into the idea."

It all came together in Seth's head. "And that's why you want to have the party?"

Marcus's face split into a grin. "You got it. And of course to make it up to Kylie."

"Of course." Seth shook his head. "How's that coming anyway?" Whatever was up between Marcus and Malcolm, he knew better than to get involved. The twins had a history, that was for sure. "Have you worked out the details with Cassidy?"

"Yup. She's good." He wiggled his eyebrows. "And a total hottie. Have you seen the ass on—"

"She's my employee."

"Doesn't mean you're blind, man."

Seth shook his head. "Whatever. But you might want to check that. I don't think you're her type, if you know what I mean?"

"What?" Seth tried to laugh at the look on his buddy's face. "You mean she's—"

"So, need anything from me?" Seth cut him off.

Marcus ran his hand through his hair in an effort to compose himself. "Only putting in a good word with Malcolm for the job."

"Right." Seth gathered up the puppies, who looked like they would happily play all day. "I'll remember that." He picked up the squirming dogs and cradled them the best he could. "So Saturday night?"

"You got it."

Seth left Marcus and safely deposited the dogs back in the maintenance shed when his cell phone vibrated in his pocket. He grabbed it and answered without looking at the call display.

"Cynthia?"

"No..."

Shit. "Malcolm. Hi." Seth ran a hand over his face. "I thought you were someone else."

"So I gather." Seth could hear the laughter in his buddy's voice. "More specifically, Cynthia. Something going on with you two?"

Clearly, as evidenced by his question, Cynthia hadn't told Kylie anything about their relationship, or Malcolm would've been the first to know about it. He knew enough about women, and more specifically, Cynthia, to know that he wasn't going to be the one to say anything. "I'm glad you called." Seth blatantly ignored the question. "There's a lot going on around here and I need you to sign off on a few things. Trent and I hammered out the details for the spring skiing package and he's already started taking reservations. When exactly are you going to be back?"

The two men segued easily into business conversation and Seth had almost forgotten about his slip answering the phone. Almost. Before he hung up, Malcolm steered the conversation back to the very subject he'd been hoping to avoid.

"Hey, speaking of Cynthia."

"We weren't."

"We sort of were," Malcolm persisted. Seth just rolled his eyes, glad the other man couldn't see his face. "Is she okay?"

Instantly, Seth was on full alert. "Why?"

"It's just that Kylie made a comment that she hadn't heard much from Cynthia lately and I know that's weird for those two. She wouldn't say anything, but I think Kylie's worried that Cynthia's upset with her for moving."

"I don't think that's it."

"I know you're not that close with her," he continued and Seth stifled a chuckle. *If Malcolm only knew.* "But do you think you could check it out for me?"

It might not be his place to say anything about the baby and their relationship, whatever it was, but Seth also couldn't outright lie to Malcolm. "You know what?" he started. "I know for a fact that Cynthia isn't upset with Kylie, but she's had a lot on her mind lately, so that's probably all it is."

"I thought you said—"

"It's her mother," Seth said. "Tell Kylie she needs to phone Cynthia. As soon as she can, okay?"

It's all he could say. But it would be enough.

WHEN THE VIBRATING of her cell phone woke her up, it was dark outside. Cynthia carefully slid off her mother's bed so she wouldn't wake her. They'd talked for hours before finally Linda couldn't keep her eyes open any longer. The conversation had taken a lot out of her, but Cynthia couldn't remember the last time she'd seen her mom so engaged. Despite the pain she was obviously in, she hadn't wanted to stop. She tucked the blankets up around her mom's tiny frame before she grabbed the phone off the side table and slipped out into the hallway.

She looked at the caller ID quickly and smiled. "Kylie. I'm glad you called."

"Is everything okay?"

Cynthia paused. She couldn't figure out an honest way to answer the question.

"Cyn?" Kylie's voice was laced with concern. "Are you okay? Your mom…is she—"

"She's fine. Well, not fine. But…" She took a deep breath before she continued. "I have so much to tell you, Kylie. I miss you so much and I know you're not really even gone yet."

"I'm never going to be totally gone." Kylie laughed. "Malcolm's doing his best to make it as easy as possible for me to get back and forth as much as possible."

"I know, but it won't be the same." Cynthia went into the kitchen and filled the kettle. "See if you can be here for a visit at the end of September, though, okay?" She smiled because Kylie wouldn't be able to guess the reason why.

"I'm sure I could try and get away, but why? Your birthday's in July."

She popped a teabag in her favorite cup and leaned against the counter. "Well, it's not exactly nine months from now, more like six, but I think it'll be someone's birthday celebration."

"What are—what? No? Who's having a baby?"

Cynthia laughed and then took a deep breath. "Me."

"What? No."

She nodded despite the fact that Kylie couldn't see her.

"You? You're…"

"Pregnant," Cynthia supplied for her. "Almost three months."

"What? I…I'm just trying…what?"

"That's kind of how I felt, too," Cynthia said. "I know it's a total shock and trust me, it wasn't planned. But now that I've had a chance to get used to the idea, I'm really happy. Scared shitless," she added. "But happy. I'm sorry I didn't tell you when we first took the test, but we just saw the doctor yesterday and you were so—"

"We?"

Cynthia swallowed hard but didn't answer right away. She'd been trying to figure out how to tell Kylie the news that not only was she pregnant but with a guy she hadn't even told her best friend about. It was a lot, especially for friends who told each other everything.

"Who's the father, Cyn? I didn't even know you were seeing anyone." The hurt in her friend's voice was clear and it hit Cynthia in the heart.

"I wasn't really seeing him. It was kind of a…" She was going to say it was a one-night stand, but it had always been more than that with Seth. Even if she didn't realize it at first. It felt wrong to belittle it to that status. "It wasn't really a planned thing," Cynthia said instead. "I didn't tell you about it because the first time was on New Year's and you were kind of…well, busy." That was an understatement: New Year's Eve was when Kylie and Malcolm had a huge blow-up fight that almost ended their relationship completely. It was definitely not the time to tell her that she'd hooked up with Seth. "And then after that, it was kind of a casual thing and when I thought I might be pregnant, well…he wanted to try dating and I think that's actually going to work out. I mean, at least for now. But I really think—"

"Cynthia! Who. Is. The. Father?"

"Seth." She held her breath and waited for the response. Cynthia had almost given up when it finally came.

"Seth?"

"Seth McBride," Cynthia confirmed.

"I had no idea you were…he's a total play—"

"No he's not." She knew exactly what Kylie was going to say and she didn't want to hear it. She'd spent too much of her own energy convincing herself that Seth wasn't a player, and he himself had made it perfectly clear that he wasn't like that. At least not anymore. She trusted him. She needed to trust him. Besides, the way he'd behaved at the doctor's appointment and then bringing her home and promising to take care of everything with the store…those were not the actions of a man who wasn't serious. Not at all. "There's a lot more to Seth than you know," Cynthia said.

Kylie was quiet for another moment but when she spoke again there was a new lightness to her voice. "So I'm going to be an auntie? The baby will call me auntie, right?"

"Of course." Cynthia laughed, relieved that Kylie was going to support her. "And you're going to have to help me pick out baby things over Skype, if you can't get back here. But it will be good to have a nurse so close by when you're finally done with school. I mean, if I'm anything like my mother says she was when I was born, I'm going to be crazy paranoid about every little hiccup. But she tells me that most new mothers are like that. So maybe it's not just her."

"How is your mom? Was she excited to hear that she's going to be a grandma?"

Tears welled in her eyes, but Cynthia blinked them back. She cleared her throat and prepared herself to tell Kylie the truth about her mother's condition and finally say out loud the one thing she hadn't even wanted to think about. Her mother wouldn't live long enough to meet her grandchild.

Chapter Twelve

FOR THREE DAYS, Seth had watched the snow fly on Stone Summit, building up the snow base and making for some of the best conditions of the entire season, tortured by the fact that he couldn't get out and enjoy the powder snow. When you were a skiing fanatic, working at a ski hill was great in theory. In fact, it always sounded like a great idea until the work actually got in the way of the skiing, and then it was just a little soul crushing. But all of that was about to change.

Because not only was Seth going to go shred some powder today, he was going to get out on the hill with Cynthia. The last few days had been hard on her, without a doubt. She'd hardly left her mother's side except to pop into the store and show Kari a few things or run out and grab some groceries. They all knew Linda didn't have much time left and everyone in Cedar Springs was being as respectful as they possibly could about it: helping out, dropping things off, or just providing an offer of support. Word about the baby seemed to have traveled as well, because not only was Cynthia receiving aid for the situation with her mother, but small gifts of prenatal vitamins, and bags of hand-me-down clothes had started to make an appearance as well. Seth had never experienced such community support before. Sure, he knew it existed, but to actually witness it in action was more than a little impressive.

But even with all the support, it was time for Cynthia to have a break. Even if it was for a few short hours. And he had a surprise for her, too. The knock on his office door signaled the arrival of either Cynthia or his surprise. Either way, he was more than ready. It continually caught him off guard with how excited he was to see the woman and make her happy. How quickly things had changed. If someone had asked him even six months ago if he could ever see himself behaving the way he was, he would have laughed at them. Or punched them in the face. Either way, he didn't care. That was before Cynthia. More and more, that was how he was defining his life these days: before Cynthia and after Cynthia.

Seth pulled the door open and seeing it was the woman he couldn't stop thinking about, he pulled her into his arms. "I'm glad you're here."

"I see that." She laughed.

"Seriously." He released her from his embrace and gave her a quick once-over. Even in her ski parka and pants, she was hotter than hell and his crotch twitched in response. But it wasn't the time nor the place, and he knew better than to even approach the subject. "I'm glad you're here. You deserve a little break and I promise it's going to be worth it."

Her face screwed up in concern as he led her outside. "I don't know, Seth. Do you think skiing is the best thing? I mean, for the baby and all? What if I fall? I don't want to fall on the baby and—"

"Dr. Gordon said it was fine. Both Dr. Gordon's, actually." He chuckled as he remembered how Cynthia had asked for a second opinion once Deanna had given her the go-ahead to ski. "They said it was fine until you were physically off balance, or uncomfortable. But even if you fall, which you won't," he added quickly, "the baby is all protected in there." He placed his hand on her abdomen and rubbed. "Besides, the fresh air will do you some good. I'm worried about you."

That made her smile. "You don't have to be worried about me. I'm fine. And you're right, this will—Oh my God, Kylie!"

Cynthia went running, as best she could in her ski boots, in the opposite direction and Seth grinned widely. "My surprise must have arrived." Malcolm and Kylie weren't due to be back in town until the following night, but Seth had arranged for them to come home early and surprise Cynthia. Not only did he think that Cynthia could use some fresh air, but he was also fairly sure she needed some best friend time as well. He turned and went to join the group.

"Good to see you, buddy." He gave Malcolm a handshake-back slap combination and gave Kylie a quick peck on the cheek. "It's good to all be together."

It was also the first time Kylie and Malcolm had seen Cynthia and Seth together as a couple, and that's what they were. At least, for lack of a better word, they were definitely a couple despite the fact that nothing had been defined. Either way, he didn't miss the looks the other couple exchanged. Seth was also very aware that the whole idea of Cynthia and him together was new for them. Hell, it was still new for him. He was beyond caring. He wrapped his arm around Cynthia and pulled her close. "Who's ready to check out the snow?"

They rode up the chairlift together on the quad chair, all sitting in a row, with Cynthia and Kylie on one side so they could catch up and Seth and Malcolm on the other. Seth figured he might as well use the opportunity to catch Malcolm up with what was going on at the hill as well. They spent the ride up lost in their separate conversations, but Seth was continually aware of Cynthia next to him. He knew she was nervous about skiing. She didn't need to be. She was an amazing skier and nothing would go wrong. But he slid his gloved hand onto her leg and squeezed, letting her know he was there. And he wasn't about to let anything happen to her. Not while he was around.

BY THE TIME they were on their third run down the hill, Cynthia was laughing as the wind whipped her face. Seth had been right. She needed a bit of fresh air. She wouldn't have traded the time with her mother for anything, but it was exhausting. They'd talked and shared and never before had Cynthia ever felt more prepared for her mother's passing, if one could ever be prepared for such a thing. But she felt as though they'd come to an understanding, and whenever it happened, she was ready.

But for the moment, Cynthia refused to think about it. She was taking Seth's advice and letting herself enjoy the afternoon. With every turn and carve of her skis, she felt a bit of the tension leave her body. All four of them skied together, carving easy *S* patterns into the fluffy snow as they went. Seth stayed a little behind her. Not enough to be annoying, or even obvious, but just enough that Cynthia knew he was looking out for her. Normally that type of thing with a man would have irritated her, but with Seth it was kind of nice to know he was protecting and looking after her. A lot of things with Seth were like that: *nice*. It surprised her how easily they were falling into a couple routine. Not that anything about them or their current situation was routine. Far from it. Every day when Seth was done with work, he went by the Store Room and made sure everything was locked up properly for the night before he came to the house. He'd bring dinner and they'd eat, all four of them, because Jess was staying over these days, in her mom's room. After dinner they'd talk, and Seth would make her mother laugh with jokes and stories about him as a young child. He'd totally won her over and when he wasn't around, she was always telling Cynthia what a good guy he was.

And he was.

She knew that now more than ever. Not only had Seth stepped up when it came to the baby, but she couldn't have asked for more support with her mom. Not only was he surprising her, she was pretty sure she was falling in love with him. If she wasn't already there. But despite how good it was, there was still that seed of doubt that she couldn't seem to shake.

"One more?"

They'd all arrived at the bottom of the hill, in a shower of snow as they stopped. Malcolm looked at them all expectantly, having asked the question.

"I'm up for it." Seth looked to Cynthia, a question in his eyes. "If you're…how are you feeling?"

Cynthia laughed. "Better than I have in a long time."

"Then it's settled," Malcolm said. "This is why I bought a ski hill in the first place."

"I thought it was for me?" Kylie smacked him in the arm with a laugh.

"No way, it was for me." They all turned and looked at Marcus, who'd appeared next to them, holding his snowboard. "Can I join you guys?"

The group glanced at each other and shrugged. "Of course." It was Seth who answered. "Just don't go shredding any of our fresh powder with your board." He punched Marcus in the arm.

"But there's too many of us for the chair." Cynthia glanced around. "Someone will have to ride—"

"No way," Kylie interrupted. "Just you and me, Cyn. Let these boys ride up together. I need some girl time with you."

It sounded like a solid plan to Cynthia, so with a wink in

Seth's direction, they pushed off and went to get in line for the chair.

THE SECOND THE safety bar was down on the chair, and they were alone, Kylie turned to Cynthia. "I like him."

"Pardon?" She'd been waiting all day for her best friend to say something about her new relationship, or situation, or whatever it was. "You what?"

"I like him, Cynthia. I've always liked Seth. He's been good to Malcolm and he's a hard worker."

And there it was. It wasn't lost on her that Kylie had conveniently left out any mention of Seth in relation to her. "That's it?"

"What else is there?"

"Seriously? Kylie." She stared at her best friend incredulously. "I just told you we were...together. It's the first time you've seen us together. I'm going to have his baby, for God's sake. I guess I thought you might have more to say."

She shrugged and looked away.

"What?"

"I don't know what you want me to say, Cyn." She turned around and faced her again. "You know I love you and I'll support you no matter what, but as much as I like Seth, I'm not sure about this. I mean, he's a nice guy. He's funny and a hard worker and good-looking."

"So what's the problem?"

"It's not that there's a problem." Kylie wouldn't meet her gaze. "So much as a concern."

"And what's that?"

"Before I say anything, I just want you to know that I do think he's a good guy and if you're happy, then I'm happy, but I am your best friend and as such, it's my job to—"

"Kylie! Just say what you need to say. I know you need to."

"He has a reputation."

Cynthia nodded and bit her bottom lip. "I know."

"It's not a secret that Seth's screwed around," Kylie said. "A lot."

"I know."

"And you're good with that?"

"God, Kylie. I screwed around with him." Cynthia laughed, but it wasn't funny. "I was one of those women who contributed to his reputation. So what exactly does that make me?"

"You're not like that."

It was true: Cynthia had always liked to party, but she'd never been the type to have random hookups with men. Until Seth, of course. But that had been different, too. It likely couldn't be considered a random hookup if you ended up in a relationship and pregnant with that man's baby. That was hardly random.

"It doesn't matter," Cynthia said instead.

"It kind of does. Are you sure you're okay with it?"

"I sort of have to be." She knew Kylie was only trying to be a good friend, but she probably didn't realize that her questions brought back a lot of the insecurities Cynthia had from day one when it came to Seth. Insecurities she thought she'd moved past. "Besides, he's been working pretty hard to prove to me he's changed."

For the next few minutes, Cynthia happily told Kylie about the romantic date Seth had planned, all the things he'd said to her, how sweet he'd been during the ultrasound, and how perfectly he'd taken care of things with the store so Cynthia could focus on her mother. By the time she was done telling Kylie everything, the worried twist in her gut had diminished again. "So you see, he's changed. A lot. All of that other stuff, that was his past. People change, Kylie. They grow up and move on. Besides, what if it just took the right woman to come along?" Those had been Seth's words and it made her all tingly inside to repeat them.

They approached the top of the chair lift, and Kylie lifted the safety bar. She gave her friend a reassuring smile and before they skied off to wait for the guys, she said, "I hope so, Cynthia. For your sake, I really hope you're right."

SETH COULD SEE the exhaustion on Cynthia's face, and when they finished the run down the hill, he called it a day. At least for them. "It was fun, guys. But I think I'm going to take the mother of my child to go visit with the puppies for a few minutes before taking her home to rest." He didn't miss the flash of smile and faint blush on Cynthia's face at his choice of words. Nor did he miss the exchange between Kylie and Malcolm. Seth knew that Kylie wasn't totally sold on him. At least not as far as dating her best friend was concerned. Not yet anyway. But she would be, because Seth didn't plan on going anywhere. Not as long as Cynthia wanted him around. And more and more every day, that situation was improving.

"I'd like to see the puppies, too." Kylie turned to Malcolm. "Maybe you should keep one. You know, to keep you company while I'm gone?"

"Don't you think I have enough on my plate just dealing with you?" He dodged her arm as it reached out to smack him and laughed. "I'm kidding." He wrapped his arms around her and gave her a kiss. "Obviously. I love dealing with you."

Marcus groaned and picked up his board. "I'm with you guys. Let's go see the puppies. Anything to get away from this."

They all laughed and headed into the maintenance shed. The moment Marcus had joined them on the hill, Seth had a feeling he was going to use the opportunity to talk to Malcolm about a job. He also knew Marcus had planned the moment

ELENA AITKEN

perfectly in order to use Seth to his advantage. Sure enough, once they were all trapped on the chairlift, Marcus had laid out his plan to work for Stone Summit and alleviate the burden on Seth while Malcolm was busy traveling back and forth visiting Kylie. Seth had to admit, Marcus laid out a pretty good case for himself and just as he'd known would happen, Malcolm turned to Seth and asked for his opinion.

He'd answered honestly. Marcus had been an asset for the last few weeks, helping out when he'd needed an extra set of hands and even taking a little initiative on his own. He still couldn't figure out what exactly Marcus was up to, and Seth knew he was up to something. It had to be more than just wanting to move home. He still couldn't buy that story. No one just wanted to leave the pro circuit behind. It didn't matter; Malcolm had agreed to give Marcus a try, just as Seth knew he would. They were twin brothers, after all. And despite the trouble in their history, that was a stronger bond than Seth would ever be able to understand.

"They're so cute." As soon as the puppies spotted them and the little balls of fluff ran toward them, Kylie dropped to her knees and gave in to the puppy kisses. "We have to keep one, Malcolm."

"What is this *we?* You won't even be here."

Kylie glared at him. "I will be eventually. Besides, this one will keep you company. She's so sweet." Kylie held out a wriggling black-and-white puppy. "We should call her Bandit."

"Isn't that a name for a boy dog?" Malcolm looked at the dog dubiously.

"No way. She's totally a Bandit. Hold her."

Reluctantly, Malcolm took the wiggly puppy from Kylie and held her out in front of him. A second later, she licked Malcolm's face and he was lost. "Okay, okay. I give in."

"We can keep her?"

"Only if we can call her something else." Malcolm looked over at the other dogs. "What are the other ones called?"

It was Cynthia who answered. "This is Nala." She scratched the dog's ears. "She's mine."

"You don't want one of the puppies?" Marcus asked. "I thought all women love puppies."

Cynthia laughed. "Who wouldn't love a puppy? But Nala and I, we're both mamas; it was meant to be." The dog looked at her with her big brown eyes and it was Seth's turn to laugh.

"It looks like she agrees."

"So you're going to let me keep her now?" Cynthia challenged him with her eyes. He'd forgotten about his little deal. But not only had she held up her end of the agreement and definitely tried letting him date her, they were so far past that now.

He stepped in close, completely unaware and uncaring about everyone watching them. "I think you know the answer to that." He pulled her in for a quick hard kiss before he stepped back with a smile.

"Well..." Marcus drew out the word. "That wasn't awkward."

Seth punched him in the arm. "Whatever."

"So what are you going to call her?" Cynthia rubbed the head of the puppy that had claimed Malcolm just as much as he'd claimed her. Maybe more. "I kind of thought they should have names that were suitable to a ski hill. Especially if you're going to keep her. It just seems right somehow."

Kylie nodded. "It does. But what's a good name?"

"What about Powder?" Marcus suggested. "We were just shredding up some pretty decent pow."

"I do not understand snowboard talk." Cynthia shook her head.

"I think we should call her Glade."

Everyone turned to stare at Malcolm.

"What kind of name is—"

"I love it." Kylie beamed and rubbed the puppy's head. "Glade because our little hideaway…" She trailed away and kissed her boyfriend so passionately, Cynthia had to look away. She caught Seth's eye and blushed. She was pretty sure he knew the story about Malcolm and Kylie's little hideaway cabin tucked into the trees right next to the out-of-bounds area of the ski hill. Kylie was right; the name Glade was perfect for the puppy.

"If it's okay with you, I think this little guy wants to come home with me." Marcus laughed at a puppy who'd attached himself to his snowboard boot. "He seems like a snowboard type. Don't you think?"

"Please tell me you aren't going to call him Shred." Cynthia reached down and pried the puppy off the boot before she handed him to Marcus.

"No way. I was thinking of Koda."

"Koda?"

"It means loyal friend."

Seth met Cynthia's eyes and he saw the worry there. She'd never been close with Marcus, especially after everything he'd put Kylie through, but it was easy to see she was worried about him anyway. Marcus's homecoming wasn't unusual. What was unusual was that he was staying home. And as far as Seth knew, he still hadn't talked to anyone about it.

"I think it's a great name," Kylie said. "But why are you getting a dog? I didn't think you'd be sticking around for long. Don't tell me we're going to inherit this dog when you decide to go back out on the circuit."

"I won't be going out on the circuit again."

Just one sentence, but it changed the whole atmosphere in the room. Someone needed to get to the bottom of whatever was going on with Marcus, but it wasn't going to be Seth. He had enough going on. "Okay," he said, breaking the tension. "That takes care of two puppies."

"What about this little one? She's so cute. This one we have to call Powder. It's a great name and she's mostly white. And come on, one of these puppies needs to be named Powder."

"I agree," Seth said. "And I know exactly who we should give her to."

Chapter Thirteen

FOR TWO DAYS after their afternoon skiing, Cynthia woke up with sore muscles. Every part of her body not only ached but throbbed. It hadn't been that long since she'd been skiing; she didn't think it was possible to be so sore from an afternoon at the hill, but with the extra hormones and all the changes flooding through her body at the moment, she no longer knew what was normal. But it had been worth it. Seth was right: getting out in the fresh air was what she needed. As was a little more sleep, but that didn't seem to be happening these days.

A wet nose nudged her hand and Cynthia lifted her head off the pillow to see Nala stare at her. "Good morning." She scratched the dog behind her ears and rolled out of bed. "Did you go out yet?"

Having never owned a dog before, Cynthia had never understood how people could talk to animals as if they would talk back. Yet in only two days, she totally got it. Having Nala around had been just what she needed, and the dog had slipped right into life in her home. For such a big dog, she was very peaceful, choosing to lie next to Linda's bedside most of the day and keep her company.

Cynthia pulled her robe on and made her way into the kitchen, where Jess was waiting the way she was every morning these days. If Cynthia didn't know better, she would think that Jess was sleeping on the couch. She stayed late and was there early, always before Cynthia woke up. She knew why, but neither of them voiced it. It was better that way.

"Good morning, Jess." Gratefully, she took the mug of tea that Jess held out for her and opened the back door for Nala. "Thank you."

"No need." Jess brushed her off. "Your mom sure likes that dog." Jess watched Nala run around the yard. "She's a perfect fit here. A better choice than a puppy. Not that they aren't cute. But, man, are they a lot of work."

Cynthia laughed and sipped at her tea. She hadn't gone with Seth to drop off the third puppy, Powder, but from everything he'd said, Kari had been thrilled to have her. Seth thought it would be a nice gesture considering Kari was helping out so much with the Store Room. And it was, in theory. But puppies were a lot of work, and from all accounts, Kari was figuring that out pretty quickly. "I heard that Kari was having fun with her new pup."

"Oh yes, she loves her," Jess said. "But from what I hear, Rhys isn't thrilled about a dog in the house. He'll melt, though. They always do. Secretly, I think all men are total suckers for animals and babies. They bring out a whole new side of even the toughest guy."

Before Cynthia could ponder how or if there would be another side to Seth when the baby came along, there was a knock on the door. "Speak of the devil."

Jess laughed as she walked over to the door. "Were we talking about him?"

"Aren't we always?" Cynthia asked as the door opened. "Good morning."

Nala walked in behind him, and Seth kicked his boots off

at the door before he walked across the kitchen to give her a kiss on the forehead. "How are you feeling this morning? Still sore?"

Cynthia stretched her arms over her head and tested her muscles. "Better. Thank you." She basked in his concern for a moment, even though she was still taken off guard every time he asked about her well-being. She wasn't used to it, but she liked it. "To what do I owe this early morning visit?"

Seth helped himself to a cup of coffee that Jess had brewed and sat across the table from her. "I'm hoping I can sway you into coming to the party tonight."

Cynthia looked down at the table and shook her head. They'd already discussed it. Leaving for the afternoon to ski was enough. Her mother's condition had only deteriorated in the past few days, and Cynthia didn't want to miss any more time with her. She wasn't going anywhere. "I told you, no."

"I know you said that but it is Kylie's going-away party and—"

"Kylie will understand."

"Of course she will." He reached across the table and took her hand. "I was thinking of you. I thought you might want to be there."

She sighed and glanced to Jess for help. Jess merely shrugged and went about preparing a breakfast tray. *A lot of help she was*. Cynthia turned back to Seth. "Of course I want to be there. But it's just a party and I can't leave my mom right now." Tears pricked at her eyes again. *Damn hormones*. She'd never in her life cried so easily. "It's just a party, Seth. We'll have another one when she comes home. We're always having parties around here. It definitely won't be the last."

"But it will be the only one where Malcolm proposes."

"What?" She slapped Seth's hand. "He's going to do what? How do you even know that? And I thought the party was supposed to be a surprise. How can he plan to propose if he doesn't even know about it?"

Seth laughed and rubbed at his hand.

"Sorry," Cynthia said sheepishly. "It was a reflex."

"It's fine. Just kind of funny."

"I'll do it again if you don't answer my questions, Seth McBride. What is going on?"

He leaned back in his chair and took an aggravatingly long sip of coffee before he answered her. "Here's the thing," he started. "It's apparently hard to keep a surprise party a surprise when the man in charge of the party looks almost exactly like the boss. One of the girls got confused and mentioned something to Malcolm about the party, thinking he was Marcus, or something like that." Seth shook his head. "Anyway, Malcolm of course asked me outright and I wasn't about to lie, so I told him."

"You told him about the surprise party?" Cynthia could think of a million ways to get out of that particular situation without revealing the truth, but maybe women were naturally more sneaky than men.

"I didn't see another choice. He is my boss, Cyn. I don't think it's a good idea to piss him off."

"Whatever." She waved her hand. "Tell me the good stuff. Malcolm's going to propose?"

Seth grinned as if he knew the world's biggest secret, which he didn't considering he'd already let it out of the bag.

"Seth, tell me." Pregnant with limited caffeine in the morning did not make a combination that Seth wanted to mess with. Even if he didn't know it yet. Fortunately for him, he was smart enough to figure it out in a hurry.

"When Malcolm found out about the party, he decided it would be a good time to propose. I guess he was planning to do it soon anyway and couldn't figure out a special way to do it, so this just worked out." Seth shrugged as if it wasn't a big deal. But it was a big deal. A very big deal.

"This is huge." Cynthia hopped up from her chair. "Does Kylie know?"

"No!" Seth was up next to her, his hands on her arms. He stared into her eyes. "And you won't tell her. Right?"

"Well, I wouldn't say anything, but you know she doesn't even know about the party and she'll want to pick out something to—"

"Cynthia." She'd never seen him look quite so serious. Well, maybe once, but that was a very different circumstance. "Tell me you won't say anything."

"Seth, I—"

"Tell me."

She swallowed hard, feeling thoroughly chastened. "Fine. I won't say anything. But why would you tell me if you didn't want me to say anything?" She knew the answer the second the question was out of her mouth. There would only be one reason Seth would break Malcolm's confidence and she shook her head even as he spoke.

"So you can be there."

"No. I told you I wasn't leaving. Mom is—"

"She'd want you to go."

Cynthia spun to look at Jess.

"I'm sorry," she said. "I couldn't help but overhear, but you know I'm right. She wouldn't want you to miss this. After all, it's Kylie."

"I know, but…what if…"

"Everything will be fine." Jess smiled and Cynthia almost believed her. "I'll stay with her. You know you should go."

Cynthia took a deep breath. She'd never forgive herself for missing Kylie's special moment, but if anything happened while she was gone…how could she live with that?

"It's up to you, babe." Seth came up behind her and

wrapped his arms around her. "Why don't you talk to your mom about it and see what she says?"

Cynthia would have laughed if she wasn't so bloody sad about everything. Seth knew damn well what her mother would say, which was exactly why he brought it up. And the fact that he knew it made her smile. He'd spent enough time with them in the last little while, that without even noticing, he'd almost become part of their little broken family. "Okay." She nodded. "I'll talk to her. But figure out Malcolm's plan, because I don't want to be gone long," she said, knowing exactly how the conversation with her mother would play out.

BY THE TIME Seth managed to get Cynthia to the party, the surprise portion of the evening was over. Once she'd agreed to come, he knew he'd be pushing it to have her there all night. So it was either the surprise, which was only really a surprise for Kylie at this point, or the proposal. It was no contest. He guided her into the lodge, which was packed with most of their friends and family. Kylie and Malcolm were the center of a small crowd off to the side of the dance floor, where people were already dancing to the pumping bass.

"Brings back memories, doesn't it?" It was in that very room where Cynthia and Seth had their first dance that led to…well, it pretty much led to their current situation. Hard to believe that was only a few months ago. He looked down at her and smiled. He wouldn't change a thing. Seth told her as much and bent down to put a kiss on her lips. "Let me get you a drink. Soda water and cran, okay?"

She nodded and forced a smile. "Sounds good."

"Go say hi to Kylie. I'll find you, okay?"

She nodded again and Seth hurried away. He knew she didn't want to be there. Her thoughts were down the mountain with her mom. But he'd been right: the moment Linda heard about the party, she'd insisted Cynthia go. She was a strong-willed woman; it was easy to see where Cynthia got it from. He'd enjoyed getting to know her over the last little while, and what had started as an effort to be there for Cynthia had quickly turned into Seth wanting to get to know Linda, and of course get the dirt on Cynthia as a little girl. The bond between mother and daughter was a strong one, and he'd picked up on it quickly. It was also why, when Cynthia had gone to lay down the night before, Seth had taken the opportunity to talk to Linda about his future with her daughter.

It was important to him that she knew how much he cared about her daughter and their unborn child.

"Mrs. Giles?" Her eyes were closed and he hadn't really wanted to bother her, but he knew he likely wouldn't get another chance to talk to her alone. "Are you sleeping?"

"Just resting my eyes." Her voice was thin and shaky, but it was threaded with a sense of humor as well. She was definitely a feisty woman.

"Can I ask you a question?"

Her eyelids fluttered open and eyes, so much like Cynthia's that it shocked him, stared directly at him. "Only if you're going to ask me about my daughter. I don't have much time for anything else."

Her frankness took him off guard, but he chuckled. "That's exactly what I'm going to ask you. I love your daughter."

"I can see that." She nodded slowly. "Does she?"

"Yes. I mean…I think so."

"Well, you've either told her or you haven't."

Chagrined, Seth shook his head. "I told her I thought I was falling in love."

"That's not the same thing."

He thought about it for a moment. "No. I guess it's not. So, the answer is, no. I haven't told her yet."

"You should. She needs to hear it." Linda closed her eyes again, and for a moment, Seth thought she might have fallen asleep. "What's your question?"

He cleared his throat and steeled himself to hear an answer he wasn't ready for. "Would you give me your blessing to marry your daughter?" The idea had only come to him that morning but once it was in his head, he couldn't get it out. It was still too soon, much too soon for him to bring it up with Cynthia, but one day he would and he wanted to make sure he'd spoken to her mother when he'd had a chance. "Not yet, I mean. But one day. When we're ready. I just wanted—"

She reached for his hand and cut him off. When she opened her eyes again, they had tears in them. "I do believe you love her, Seth. You'll be good to her and good for her."

"I will." He nodded and let her continue.

"She's a stubborn girl." Seth fought the urge to laugh. Boy, did he know that firsthand. "Make sure she knows you love her."

He'd nodded as if he understood, but then changed his mind and asked, "And how do I do that?"

She'd laughed then, the first time Seth had ever heard it. It was short and when she stopped, she squeezed his hand again. Harder than he thought possible. She looked straight into his eyes. "I'd suggest you start by telling her."

AND THAT'S EXACTLY what he planned to do tonight. Seth glanced over his shoulder to see Cynthia had made her way into the crowd to give Kylie a hug. Yes, he was definitely telling her exactly how he felt tonight. Just as soon as Malcolm had his moment. But first, he was going to get her a drink and make sure she relaxed as much as possible for one evening. Lord knew Cynthia deserved a little bit of fun.

"A soda with cran," he told the bartender. "And a...actually, make it two."

"A show in solidarity, I presume?"

Seth turned and broke into a smile when he saw Deanna next to him. "Dr. Gordon. That's exactly what it is." He laughed. "What about you—can I get you something to drink?"

"Call me Deanna," she said with a smile of her own. "And yes, I'd love a glass of white wine."

"One wine, coming up." Seth got the bartender's attention and ordered the drink. "It's nice to see you," he said. "Outside of the office, that is. But I suppose you know a lot of this group, too."

"I do." Together they turned and surveyed the room. "It's funny how many people change and yet remain the same all at the same time."

"That's the beauty of a small town, isn't it?"

"I suppose it is."

"So you're glad to be back?"

Her face changed and the smile slipped away. "I'm not back. I'm just visiting."

Seth didn't have a chance to ask her what she meant by that because their drinks arrived. He paid the bartender and was ready to excuse himself and find Cynthia, whom he no longer saw with Kylie. He scanned the room quickly, but still couldn't see her. Kylie was back at Malcolm's side and they'd made their way to another group of friends.

"Deanna, you'll have to—"

"Hey buddy."

Marcus slapped him on the back and Seth moved quickly to keep his drinks from splashing onto Deanna. "Hey." He looked to Deanna, who he'd fortunately missed. "Sorry about that," he said.

She shook her head. "That's okay." Her voice was tight and

her mouth pressed into a thin line as she stared at the interruption.

Seth turned to Marcus. "What the hell, man?"

"Oh, my bad." Marcus grinned and Seth shook his head. He knew exactly what his friend was up to. A little charm always did seem to get him out of trouble. He pushed past Seth and held out his hand. "I'm so sorry. I'm Marcus."

She didn't take his hand, but glared up at him. "I know who you are."

Without missing a beat, Marcus slid his hand through his hair. "You do look familiar. I must have seen you around. Are you a snowboarding fan, then?"

"Hardly." Deanna scoffed and Seth laughed. As entertaining as this was bound to get, he needed to find Cynthia.

"Well, I'd love to stick around," he said, mostly to Deanna. "But I really do have to find Cynthia."

"I saw her talking to Samantha a few minutes ago," Marcus volunteered. He eyed Deanna strangely, no doubt trying to figure out whether he knew her or not. And what exactly he'd done to her to earn the cold shoulder she was giving him. With Marcus, it could be anything. But Marcus and Malcolm hadn't grown up in Cedar Springs, they'd come later, so there was a good chance his path hadn't crossed with the good doctor. Seth shook his head. It was a mystery for another day.

"It was good to see you, Deanna. Have a—"

"Deanna!" Marcus blurted out. "Holy shit, it's...wow...you look so..."

Marcus had obviously connected the dots to their past, but judging by the look on Deanna's face, Seth wasn't going to hang around to bear witness to whatever fireworks were bound to come out of that particular reunion.

CYNTHIA HAD TO ADMIT, she was having a good time. It was probably a good thing that she'd come. Although, after she had made her round of the room talking to all her friends and a healthy share of nosy acquaintances and answering all their questions about Seth and the baby, she was growing weary. She'd happily head home to check on her mother, but not only had Malcolm not popped the question to Kylie, Cynthia couldn't see him anywhere.

"Hey beautiful." Seth slid his arm around her, and pulled her into an embrace. She was still getting used to being with him in public, or really with him at all. She knew they were getting looks from people. More specifically, women he'd had wild one-night stands with. She tried to ignore their stares, and focus on the man in front of her, but every once in a while she'd lock eyes with some girl who clearly thought they might have had a chance with Seth McBride, and all the old feelings of insecurity and doubt flooded back.

He kissed her, and she forced her body to relax into the moment and stop worrying about what anyone else thought. "Can we get out of here soon? This is exhausting."

He kept his arms around her, but pulled back enough to look into her eyes. "The partying getting to you? It is hard to be the only one not drinking in a room like this." He laughed. "It's kind of—"

"It's not that."

"Then what?" He turned his head and followed her gaze to a blond woman she didn't recognize on the other side of the room who'd been staring at them for the past few minutes. "Ah, that."

"Yes. That."

Seth turned and focused only on her again. "That's nothing. She's nothing."

"Then why does she keep glaring at me like she'd like to—"

"It doesn't matter." He kissed her. "I'm with you. I'm only with you, and my past is just that. My past. Remember?"

"I'm trying."

His hands found her hips; his fingers slid down to cup her bottom. "Does this help?" Lust danced in his eyes, and despite her misgivings, Cynthia found herself focusing less on the woman across the room, and much more on the man in front of her. "What about this?" Seth dropped his lips to her neck and found the sensitive spot right by her collarbone.

"Oh, I think that might help." She closed her eyes, completely uncaring that they were in the middle of a busy party where anyone could see. What did it matter anyway? Let people think what they were going to think.

"Dance with me."

"What?" Her eyes flew open. "What was wrong with—"

"Come on. I like this song."

She liked the song, too. Ed Sheeran's "Thinking Out Loud" was a gorgeous song. A little strange for a party setting, but who cared? She let Seth lead her out to the dance floor, where a number of other couples already swayed to the music.

Seth was a good dancer. Just another thing she was learning about him, and liking. In fact, more and more, Cynthia found herself liking most of the things she learned about Seth McBride. She closed her eyes and let him lead her expertly around the dance floor.

She lost herself in the lyrics of the song and it took her a moment to realize Seth was singing to her.

She opened her eyes. His voice was low so no one but her could hear.

"This song is perfect for us," he said when he realized she was watching him. "I kind of think we found love in mysterious ways."

Seth swung her around again and Cynthia tucked her head

onto his shoulder. When he sang the next lyrics about finding love right where they were, her breath hitched.

They were just lyrics to a song, but the way he looked at her when he sang them spoke directly to her heart.

"Seth, did you just…"

He smiled and nodded slowly. "Cynthia, there's been something I've been meaning to—"

A collective gasp rose up from the crowd and for a second, Cynthia thought it was because of what Seth was obviously about to say to her, but then she realized the music had stopped, and the dance floor had cleared; everyone looked directly at Malcolm, who was down on one knee in front of Kylie.

Cynthia squealed and clapped her hand over her mouth, rushing over to make sure she saw the moment.

"Kylie Wilson," Malcolm was saying. "I've been in love with you from the moment I first laid eyes on you, right here at this ski hill. I knew then that you'd be the woman to complete me and it may have taken a bit longer to come to our happy ending than I would have liked, but I wouldn't change any of it because everything we've been through has made us who we are today." Cynthia was vaguely aware of Seth's arms wrapping around her, as he pulled her back to him while they watched the proposal. She rested her head on his chest and continued to listen. "You've always made me want to be a better man. Because of you, your love and support, I've been able to achieve more than I could ever have imagined. And now, as you set off to follow your dreams, I want nothing more than to be the man at your side, supporting you and loving you as you achieve everything your heart desires." Kylie's shoulders shook with emotion, and Cynthia bit her lip to keep from crying for her best friend. "Kylie, would you do me the honor of allowing me to forever walk by your side? To be your strength as you are mine? To be the other half of my heart?

Kylie, will you be my wife?" He pulled out a ring box and flipped it open as he spoke.

As Malcolm finished his speech, the room grew quiet as he waited for Kylie's answer. And then she nodded, so slightly, it would have been easy to miss, and the word "yes" was lost in a chorus of whistles and hoots as Malcolm put the ring on her finger, jumped to his feet and lifted Kylie, spinning her around. A tear leaked from Cynthia's eye and she couldn't wipe it fast enough before Seth noticed. He spun her around so she faced him.

"He did a good job." He gently wiped the tear from her cheek. "I'm impressed. Who knew Malcolm had it in him?"

She smacked his arm half-heartedly. "Some men are romantic," she teased, but as soon as the words were out of her mouth, she remembered the extremely romantic date he'd planned for her. "I mean, you were. I mean, you—"

"Cynthia, I know." Seth placed a finger on her lips to silence her. "We got interrupted earlier, but there was something I wanted to say to you."

She nodded, the crowded room falling away as she only focused on the man in front of her.

"I've been waiting to tell you that," he swallowed hard, and something low in her gut tugged at his vulnerability, "Cynthia, I—"

"Cynthia!" A hand on her arm yanked her around and out of Seth's private embrace. It took her half a second to focus on Kari Fox, who stood in front of her, a cell phone in her hand and a look on her face that told Cynthia everything before she even spoke the words. "It's your mom. You have to get home."

Chapter Fourteen

THEY HELD the funeral service three days later, on a warm, almost spring-like afternoon. She couldn't be sure whether she was just in shock, or whether she really was handling everything okay. Cynthia sat through the service, Seth at her side, and managed to hold herself together. Mostly. When they played the slideshow that Cynthia and Linda had put together only a few weeks earlier, she let the tears slide down her cheeks unchecked. Pictures and memories of her mother as a young woman, and then a young mother with Cynthia at her side, flashed across the screen while "Somewhere Over The Rainbow" played in the background.

She cried over the memories, including the most recent one of them choosing the pictures for the very slideshow she was now watching. She cried for what she'd lost, and as the final picture of her mother taken only a few months earlier, at Christmas, slid across the screen, she cried for what her unborn child had lost. A family.

Later, as she stood at the door and accepted condolences from friends and townspeople, Cynthia kept going back to that thought. Now, with her mother gone, she was all alone. She'd never known her father, and as an only child, there was no sibling to lean on. Sure, there were aunts and uncles. Somewhere. They were such distant relations that they didn't bother making the trip to the funeral. They could hardly be considered family. No. It was just her now. And the baby.

"Cynthia?" Seth's voice startled her out of her thoughts and she realized she'd been staring at Lorne, who'd been her mother's account manager at the bank, for far too long. Had her mother even known him beyond business? "Cynthia?" Seth said her name again. "Maybe you should come sit down for a minute."

It wasn't a question or a request, because before she could even nod, she felt herself being led away. "Thank you for coming," she said reflexively to Lorne before she went with Seth.

"I'm fine." She tried to brush Seth's hands away as they guided her to a chair. "I need to go thank everyone."

"No you don't." Seth pushed a bottle of water into her hand. "They all know you appreciate them coming. There's no need to stand there and torture yourself like that. I've never understood that part of funerals. It's ridiculous."

Cynthia took a sip from the bottle and watched Seth pace in front of her. There was nothing funny about the situation, yet she felt laughter bubble up inside her throat as she watched him rant about funeral etiquette.

"All you really need to do is say goodbye to your mother," he was saying. "You don't need any of this bullshit that goes along with it." He stopped abruptly and dropped to his knees in front of her. "How are you feeling? Are you tired? You haven't been sleeping very well." A fact he only knew because he hadn't left her side, practically moving in with her, taking care of every detail without being asked. If anyone needed sleep, it was probably him, but Cynthia didn't say anything. "If you need to lie down, we can sneak away. I'm sure everyone will—"

"I'm not an invalid," she snapped. And then softening her voice because he was only trying to be helpful, she added, "Seriously, Seth, I'm fine. Thank you for everything you've done for me, but I'm okay." He looked at her suspiciously. "Honestly. I'm fine. It's like I've been preparing for this for months, you know? It's probably..." She sniffed hard and swiped at her eyes. "No," she tried again. "It is better this way. I know she's in a better place now. She's not hurting anymore." Cynthia took a deep breath and exhaled slowly, allowing herself a moment to compose herself before she stood up. "Funerals are really more for the living, don't you think?" She took another sip of water and handed the bottle back to Seth. "I mean, really. It's not like Mom knows anyone is here crying over her. The whole thing is—"

"Cynthia." He grabbed her arm to stop her from leaving. "It's okay to be sad. To let yourself feel something. You don't have to be strong through this. No one expects you to."

It was the right thing to say, at completely the wrong time. She'd been doing her best to hold everything together. There was no doubt if she let herself, she'd unwind completely because even when you had time to *prepare*, there was no way you could actually prepare for the loss of your mother. She clenched her fists to keep her hands from shaking as a flood of emotion washed through her body. "You don't think I'm feeling anything?"

"No...I..." He stumbled over his words. "That's not what I was saying."

"I know exactly what you were saying." Logically, she knew that he didn't deserve her rage but she couldn't help it. She needed a release, and he was the unfortunate target. "I feel a lot of things, Seth McBride. I feel sad—no." She shook her head. "Sad isn't the right word. How do you adequately describe losing the only person in your life who loved you just for being you? I feel crushed, devastated, completely shredded from the inside out because she's gone. Is that what you want to hear?" The tears flowed freely down her face as she continued. "Do you want to hear how as I held her hand and watched her take her last breath I felt a piece of myself die too? Do you want to hear that? Because the minute her spirit left this earth, so did everything I know." Her hands went numb and she could feel her body vibrate as she spoke, but she couldn't stop. "I am *feeling*, Seth. A lot. I'm feeling angry that she's gone. Relieved that she's not in pain anymore. Ripped off that she never got to meet her grandbaby. And more than anything, I'm feeling completely fucking terrified, because now I'm all alone in the world. But I don't have the luxury right now to let myself really feel any of those things, because whether you understand it or not, I have a room full of people who have come to pay their respects and I know my mother wouldn't want me to be rude. So I'm feeling like you need to butt out and mind your own business. So, yes. I'm feeling a few things."

She stalked off, leaving Seth with his mouth open and staring after her. She knew he didn't deserve any of it and the second the words were out of her mouth, the guilt took over. But she didn't have time for guilt and she definitely didn't have time to feel bad about it. She could add both things to the growing list of things she was feeling, and had no clue how to deal with.

HE LET HER GO. Her words stung a little—hell, more than a little—but Seth also knew that none of them were aimed at him. Not directly anyway. Cynthia needed space to grieve and feel all the things she was feeling and by the sounds of it, she was feeling quite a bit. He sank into the chair she'd vacated moments before and gave himself a break. He was exhausted and no, it wasn't the same thing as what Cynthia was going through. Not even close, but the last few days had taken a toll on him, too.

From the second they'd been interrupted at the party by the phone call from Jess, everything had sped up to warp speed, moving so quickly, he could barely keep up. And yet, at the same time it felt as though the days had played out in slow motion. Thank goodness Jess had known Linda well enough and spent enough time with her to recognize that something was different that night. She'd tried to call Cynthia, but when she hadn't been able to reach her, she'd started to call friends and had finally caught Kari.

Seth had taken Cynthia straight home, where she hadn't left Linda's side. It hadn't taken long and all Seth could think was thank God he'd gotten her there in time. She never would have forgiven herself, or him, if she hadn't been with her mother at the end.

"Hey." Kylie sat down next to him. He hadn't even seen her walk up. He nodded in response. "I thought I might find you here."

"You did?" He scrubbed his hand over his face. "How is that?"

"Well, not here necessarily." She shrugged. "But close by. When I saw Cynthia alone, I figured you had to be nearby. You haven't left her side in days," she said. "How are you doing?"

"It's not about me."

"You know what I meant."

Seth turned to look at Kylie. He'd never really spent much time with her. Sure, they'd known each other and then as Malcolm's girlfriend, they'd spent a bit of time together, but he could hardly say they were close friends. Yet…he did know what she meant and suddenly the idea of denying he was feeling anything exhausted him. "I'm tired," he said honestly. "But it doesn't matter, and you and I both know that."

Kylie nodded. "I know."

They sat in silence for a few minutes and even though they didn't speak, Seth drew energy from her presence.

When Kylie spoke again, she took him off guard. "Don't let her push you away, okay?"

He turned and raised an eyebrow in question.

"Do you care about her?" Kylie asked point-blank. She shifted in her chair so she faced Seth.

"Of course," he said. "I…" He drifted off, aware that he'd never had the chance to tell Cynthia how he really felt. He'd been about to have a moment with her on the dance floor, a perfect romantic moment that had twice been interrupted. Ever since, it hadn't felt appropriate to share his feelings and he sure as hell wasn't about to tell her best friend before he told Cynthia. "I do," he finished lamely.

Kylie narrowed her eyes, obviously aware that he wasn't saying everything. Thankfully, she didn't push him. "From what I can see, you do," she said. "And I know the timing sucks and you both have a few things to deal with."

That was putting it mildly, but Seth didn't say anything.

"I know Cynthia better than anyone," she continued. "She's hurting right now."

"That's understandable."

"Of course it is. But that just means now, more than ever, she needs to know you care."

"She does." Seth spoke before thinking and then remembering the way Cynthia had just lashed out at him, he added, "At least I think so."

Kylie's smile was warm as she stood and straightened her dress. "I think you're a good guy, Seth."

"Thanks."

She laughed a little before her face changed again. "Seriously, don't let her push you away."

Kylie turned and walked away before Seth could say anything else. Her words rang in his ears long after she was gone. One thing he was sure of: Cynthia could push all she wanted, but he wasn't going anywhere.

THE REST of the day passed in a blur of well wishes, wrapped casseroles, and flowers and finally, blissfully, Cynthia closed the door on the last guest, and she was alone. She leaned back against the door and dropped her head to her chest. The house was quiet. Too quiet. Somehow a house that was empty by choice felt differently than one that was empty due to circumstance. It had been exhausting trying to hold it together and keep a smile on her face all day, and she'd done nothing but wish it was over. After her outburst, Seth had kept his distance, but he'd still been close by until finally she'd sent him away, too. He hadn't wanted to go, creating a dozen reasons he should stay, but she'd insisted. And now that she was finally alone, the quiet she'd craved smothered her. She closed her eyes and tried to breathe through the sensation.

She didn't know how long she stood there, taking one slow, deep breath after another as she tried to figure out what to do next. She heard Nala rise from her blanket next to the couch. The dog's nails clicked on the hardwood floor moments before she nudged her wet nose against Cynthia's hand. She wasn't alone. Cynthia crumpled to the floor, wrapped her arms around the dog and sunk her face into Nala's soft fur while she sobbed.

The dog had been a lifesaver over the last few days. It was amazing how much she'd come to depend on Nala and how the dog had become such an important part of her life so quickly. Just like the man who'd given her the dog.

Seth.

And she'd pushed him away. She'd said terrible things to him, most of which she hadn't meant. And even the things she had meant, they shouldn't have been directed at Seth. It wasn't his fault. Cynthia lifted her head and sniffed loudly as she swiped at her tears. Nala licked her face, which made her laugh a little.

"I've been such a bitch, Nala." The dog tilted her head and whined. "You think so, too, huh?"

"I don't think so."

Cynthia whipped her head around to see Seth under the arch between the kitchen and the living room with a large paper bag in his hands.

"I hope you don't mind, but I came in the back door."

Nala ran over to greet him, leaving Cynthia alone in the middle of the floor on her knees. "I thought I asked you to leave me alone tonight?" She sounded like such a bitch and she hated it, but she couldn't seem to stop herself.

"You did."

She pushed herself up off the floor and tugged at her dress, which had been stretched awkwardly over her tummy bulge all day. "Then why are you here?" A battle waged inside her even as she spoke the words. Her heart had leapt at the sight of him and the urge to sit with him—a welcome comforting presence —was strong. She didn't want to be alone. Not really. But she also didn't want him to be there only because he felt sorry for her or felt a sense of obligation or any of the other thousands of reasons she'd created in her head. Things with Seth were already complicated; she didn't need to add pity to the list of complications.

"I brought dinner." He put the bag on the side table before he walked across the room to her. "I thought you'd be hungry."

He didn't touch her, but he stood so close she could feel the heat from his body.

"I have a kitchen full of lasagnas and chicken casseroles."

"Then we can eat that."

"I don't want to eat that," she snapped. She couldn't think straight. His proximity messed with her head and made it hard to think. Her body naturally leaned toward him, wanting to be in his arms to seek the comfort she knew he could offer. But another part of her knew she needed to protect herself.

"Cynthia." His voice was low and enticing. "I'm not leaving." He reached out and trailed one finger down her cheek; her heart went into overdrive. She squeezed her eyes shut against the assault of sensations that flowed through her at the one simple touch.

Dammit.

Maybe it was the buildup of emotions over the last few weeks, and days especially. Maybe it was the way he looked at her. Maybe it was that she'd somehow dropped her guard, just enough. Whatever it was, in that moment, everything crystallized. Despite herself, she was totally and completely in love with this man. And that scared the hell out of her. It was too much to handle.

Cynthia bit her bottom lip and turned away. "You should go." Without looking back, she walked down the hall. She flinched as she passed her mother's shut door. She needed the day to be over. All she wanted was to put her sweatpants on and crawl into her bed and forget about everything. She reached in vain around her back and then over her shoulder in an attempt to grab the zipper on the back of the dress. Dammit. Seth had been there earlier, when she'd gotten dressed. Like every morning for the last few days, she'd woken up next to him and they'd slipped into an easy routine as he helped her with the less than easy days.

He'd zipped her up into the dress. An act that had been so

familiar and easy. Why was it suddenly so hard to imagine him there with her? Her brain swirled and nothing made sense. Yes, she wanted him, but she knew her heart couldn't take any more hurt. She couldn't risk it.

"Let me help you." He was behind her; his hand gently swept her hair off her back and to one shoulder as the other eased the zipper down. The gentle touch almost cracked her. Seth's hand slipped beneath the fabric and skimmed down her back.

"Seth." She shook her head slightly.

"Cynthia." He kissed the base of her neck. "I thought we were past all this. Let me help you."

They both knew he wasn't talking about her dress any longer.

He turned her in his arms, so he was encasing her. "What's changed?" His eyes were so intense, the way they held her, and saw right into her soul and all the war that waged within her.

"Everything," she whispered. She closed her eyes against the onslaught of his stare. "She's gone." The words came out so quietly she wasn't even sure herself that she'd spoken aloud. "She's really gone and...I don't know how to..."

"I know." Seth pulled her tight, not allowing her to escape again while she cried. "I know," he said again and again while he stroked her hair, smoothing it down her back, and allowed her the freedom to cry.

When Cynthia was sure she couldn't cry anymore, the tears would start fresh. But not once did he rush her, or try to offer any other words of comfort. He simply held her. It was perfect. It was enough. Finally, the tears dried and, feeling as if she'd been wrung out, she lifted her head from his chest. His t-shirt was soaked through, and with one finger she traced the wet spot over his heart. "I'm sorry."

"Don't be." He caught her hand and folded her fingers into his own. "Never be sorry for what you feel." He kissed her hand. "And judging by everything you told me earlier, you're feeling a whole hell of a lot right now."

She blushed; the heat of her mortification flooded her face. She'd really let loose on him and although he hadn't deserved the brunt of her emotional outburst, she'd needed the release. "Okay, but I am sorry about that," she tried to apologize. "You've been nothing but great during all of this and you didn't—"

"I told you not to apologize, remember?" He smiled, and it did something wicked to her insides. "But you were wrong about one thing."

Her eyes flicked up, curious. "I wasn't—"

"You were." Seth threaded his fingers through hers, and held her hands at her sides. "Earlier, you said you were alone now. But you were wrong." She opened her mouth, but he didn't give her the chance to speak. "You, Cynthia Giles, are the furthest thing from being alone." With his hand still entwined in hers, he moved it to her stomach. "There's the baby."

"But that—"

He silenced her with a tip of his head and moved his other hand, still holding hers, to his chest. "And there's me. Do you feel that? That beat?"

She bit her bottom lip and nodded.

"You are far from alone. Because right here, the three of us?" She stifled a sob, but he continued. "Together, we are a family. We're your family, Cynthia. How can you possibly be alone surrounded by this love?"

Love? Never had they spoken of love, except for that moment in the hot tub, but that wasn't the same thing. God, she wanted him to say it. From the moment she even suspected that's what she'd felt for Seth, she'd only wanted him to just come out and tell her. Old-fashioned? Maybe, but it wasn't about that. It was about...

"Stop thinking." He interrupted her internal dialogue as if he knew she was overanalyzing everything. Which she was. "Just feel, Cynthia. Because dammit, I'm so sick of thinking about this. I just need to say it already." He tilted her chin up and put his hands on either side of her face to hold her. "Cynthia, I knew that it was going to be a good year for me because the moment I held you in my arms for the first time and tasted your lips on mine that night, I was lost to you. Everything in the last few months has just been me trying to get out of my own way and realize just how much you mean to me. You stole my heart on New Year's Eve and God help me, but I don't want it back." He smoothed his thumb over her lips, bent in and whispered, "I love you," before he kissed her thoroughly.

It was everything she'd needed to hear and more. The moment the words left his mouth, they resonated with something deep inside her and broke down the last of the walls that barricaded her heart.

"Seth?"

"You're not going to tell me you don't feel the same way, are you?" He gave her a half smile. "Because if you do, I won't recover from it."

She smiled. "No." She shook her head. "No, I'm not going to say that, because dammit if I haven't fallen in love with you, too."

He grinned and his eyes sparkled with it. "You say that like it's a bad thing."

"It's not." She smacked him lightly on the chest and he caught her wrists in his again, pinning her to him and sending a shot of desire right to her core. She could feel his need pressed up against her belly. "It's not bad at all." Her voice came out in a husky breath.

Seth backed her up slowly until her legs hit the mattress and she sat down on the bed. "What was it you were going to say then?" He bent and nipped at her neck; thrills shivered through her body. She arched into the sensation while he pushed her dress down off her shoulders. His kisses traveled down between her breasts, when he looked up expectantly for the answer to his question.

"It can wait."

His smile was wicked, but he moved up so he hovered over her again. His voice was full of the love he felt for her when he said, "That's good. Because we've got the rest of our lives. And this is going to take awhile."

Epilogue

A FEW WEEKS LATER...

SPRING MIGHT HAVE STARTED to bloom down the mountain in Cedar Springs, but even in the third week of April there was still decent snow at Stone Summit and with the sun shining, the conditions would be perfect for the Slush Cup that was only a few days away. It would be the perfect way to end the season, and not a moment too soon. Seth loved running the ski hill, but now with Cynthia, and the baby on the way. Well, he could think of other things he was going to be busy with.

Not for the first time, he reminded himself what a good idea it had been to hire Marcus Stone to help at the hill. Especially with Malcolm so preoccupied with Kyle in Vancouver, his twin brother would be a welcome addition.

A fact that Marcus never hesitated to remind them of. Seth shook his head and laughed at himself as the man walked toward them, tossing snowballs for the dog that happily bounded after each one.

Marcus threw another snowball for the dog, this time dangerously close to Seth.

"Hey." Seth caught the snow and fired it back at Marcus, who dodged it easily. "Careful, you almost hit the mother of my child and for that, there would have been serious consequences."

Marcus bowed dramatically as he neared the couple. "Sorry, Cynthia. You know I'd never hit you."

She laughed and smacked Seth. "I know it. How are you, Marcus?"

"Keeping busy. There's lots going on, you know?" He looked right at Seth when he said that, not that he needed to remind the man any more that even though his life had taken a turn, he still had a ski hill to run. It was true, he'd been the one reluctant to hire Marcus, and it wasn't lost on him that now it was Marcus saving his ass while he was out taking baby appointments and shopping for strollers. "How was the appointment?" Marcus asked. "Everything good with baby McBride?"

Cynthia shot Seth a look. "McBride? I thought—"

"I think that's a conversation for later." Seth took her hand and gave her a kiss on the cheek. It was a momentary respite for the conversation they'd have to have later, but Seth didn't doubt for a moment that it wouldn't end up with the two of them in each others arms laughing and kissing and...

FOR A SPLIT SECOND, Marcus felt something like regret as he watched the couple. Not that he had any interest in being a father, or having a woman so obviously in charge of him. No way. He needed that like he needed another hole in his head, and that was definitely not on the agenda. "But it was a good appointment." Seth directed the conversation back into safer ground. "We found out the sex of—"

"We're having a girl!"

"Whoa." Seth shook his head and laughed. "So much for the gender reveal party you were talking about."

"I couldn't help it." Cynthia oozed excitement and despite the fact that Marcus could really care less about what sex their baby was, he actually found himself smiling along with her.

"That's awesome," he said, and meant it. He may not care about what sex their baby was, but Cynthia had become a friend, and she'd been through a lot with the loss of her mother. If she was happy, he was happy. He gave her a quick hug and then excused himself.

"I'm happy for you guys, I really am. But I do have a lot of work to do. The Slush Cup is next week already, and—"

"I know, I know," Seth interrupted him. "And you have a lot of work to do. We do appreciate you helping out so much with this, Marcus. It couldn't have come at a better time."

He tried not to bristle at Seth's choice of words. He was more than helping out, but there was no point in mentioning it. He was just about to turn and head into the offices when he heard a familiar voice. A voice he'd both wanted to avoid and to hear again since he'd run into her at the party a few weeks ago. How the hell he hadn't recognized her then, he had no idea. It had taken years to get her out of his head the first time. He froze, torn between wanting to see her and knowing it wasn't a good idea. Maybe she'd pass by.

"Hi guys. I'm glad I caught you."

No such luck.

He put the biggest, most charming smile on his face and turned to greet the woman. "Hi, Deanna."

Her big beautiful smile faltered when she saw it was him. No doubt she'd thought it was Malcolm who stood next to Cynthia and Seth. A thought that was only confirmed by her next words. "Oh, Marcus. I didn't think...I thought you were—"

"Malcolm? Sorry to disappoint." He knew it was an asshole thing to say, especially to Deanna. God, anything was an asshole thing to say to Deanna. At least that's how she would see it, of that he had no doubt.

"Yes," she muttered. Her face turned a shade of red that he would have found attractive in any other situation. Hell, he found it hot even given the situation they were in. Which was awkward to say the least. "I meant, no. I meant... Never mind."

Seth and Cynthia exchanged a look with each other that Marcus pretended not to notice. He shook his head clear of any further urge to get her worked up, and there was definitely an urge there, and tried again. "I know what you meant," he said agreeably. "It's an easy mistake."

"Right," Cynthia jumped in. "Well, anyway, I'm glad you could come, Deanna. When you said it had been years since you'd been on the hill, I knew we had to fix that at once."

"And by fix it," Seth said, "she means, make it her personal mission to get you out here."

"Well, I want to try to convince Deanna to stay in Cedar Springs long term."

"You're not staying?" He couldn't help it. Marcus knew he should just ignore the conversation, and definitely not engage her, but the disappointment he felt hearing she'd be leaving was real.

She focused her dark eyes on him, and his entire body reacted hard and fast to her stare. There was a time when he would have been able to read what she was thinking. Not anymore. She was a closed book. One he'd once enjoyed reading. But that was in the past. Where it needed to stay. They'd shared an incredible two weeks together a few years ago right after she'd graduated from medical school. Or, more specifically they'd spent two weeks sneaking around together when she'd been home for Christmas holidays. If he remembered correctly, her eyes had been full of passion back then. Maybe they were just that much easier to read when she was beneath him, making her moan?

"No, I'm not." Deanna crossed her arms across her chest. "It's temporary. I'll be getting out of here just as soon as I can."

"But in the meantime," Cynthia jumped in, "I'm going to convince her to stay and that starts with some time on the hill."

Marcus shifted uncomfortably. He could see exactly where the conversation was going and he didn't think it was a good idea to stick around for it. "I should probably get going."

"No, wait." Cynthia put her hand on his arm. "I'm actually glad we ran into you. We were going to take Deanna out on the hill, but now that I'm in my second trimester, I don't feel comfortable skiing anymore. And as it turns out, Deanna doesn't ski, she—"

"Snowboards." Marcus stared straight at Deanna, who had returned to trying to ignore him. "I remember."

"Right." Cynthia glanced between them. "I keep forgetting that you two know each other."

"We don't really—"

"We only met the—"

They both spoke at the same time before they broke off and stared at each other. She was every bit as beautiful as he remembered. More so. Years ago, he'd met a girl and now there was no denying a woman stood before him.

"Okay, well…" Cynthia broke the silence but still they didn't break their gaze. "Then this will work out perfectly," Cynthia continued. "Deanna said it had been so long since she'd been snowboarding that she could benefit from a lesson, but all the boarding instructors are booked up with spring break lessons, so…"

Deanna shook her head; her thick, black braid swayed across her back and all Marcus could think of was how he'd like to wrap his hand around it and pull those full pouty lips to his and kiss all of their memories away. Or reignite them.

No. That was never going to happen. Never again. But it wouldn't hurt to spend one afternoon with her. Would it?

"I'll do it," he said, almost before he realized he'd spoken. Her eyes flew up to meet his, but he ignored the question he saw there. "I can't think of a better way to spend the afternoon than to reintroduce Deanna to the board."

"And I can't think of a better person to do it." Cynthia smiled.

Still he didn't take his eyes from her. His gaze dared Deanna to object. He knew she wouldn't. "Neither can I."

What kind of history do Marcus and Deanna share? Will they be able to deny their chemistry? Do they really want to?
Find out in Summit of Passion
You can read an exclusive excerpt right after this——
>

I appreciate you helping me spread the word about the books you love! Reviews help readers discover their next favorite read! Please leave a review on your favorite book retailer!

Don't forget to join my mailing list where you'll be the first to hear about new stories, sales and promotions and giveaways!
You can join me here —>
https://elenaaitken.com/newsletter/

Summit of Passion

Please enjoy this exclusive excerpt of Summit of Passion!

Maybe there would be a medical emergency? Maybe, if she got lucky, someone would have a heart attack and she'd be called down to town. Deanna Gordon shook her head and mentally scolded herself. No. That wasn't okay. It was never okay to wish someone ill health. Even if it would be a good excuse to get her off the ski hill and away from Marcus Stone, who currently walked toward her, his snowboard casually hefted over his shoulder and looking so damn sexy that it interfered with Deanna's ability to think straight.

If she could just think of something—*anything*—to get out of the afternoon snowboarding lesson from Marcus. She just couldn't seem to make her brain work fast enough to come up with a plausible explanation for blowing off the very generous gift from Seth McBride and her old friend Cynthia Giles. Ever since she returned to Cedar Springs about a month ago, she'd been their doctor and had been the one to officially declare Cynthia pregnant. Being able to see one of her oldest friends through such a special experience was definitely one of the perks of being a doctor in her hometown. It may be the only perk that she could think of. And there were definitely drawbacks, and the biggest one stood in front of her with a killer smile and a look in his eyes that had never before failed to make her stomach flip.

"Ready to do this?"

It was too late. She couldn't think of a damn thing to say to get her out of it. Not without looking like a total bitch, anyway. "Absolutely." She gave him her sweetest smile. Maybe if she faked her way through the afternoon, it would go faster. Besides, if she remembered correctly, she wasn't the only one who was affected by spending time in close proximity together. The way she remembered it, their connection had been very much a mutual thing.

"You got a rental board?" Marcus bent down to pick up her snowboard from where it rested at her feet. "What happened to yours?"

"How do you know it's not mine?"

"Your board used to have those big pink flowers all over it." He smiled when he spoke, and damned if it didn't send thrills right through her. She wasn't supposed to be so affected by him.

"That was years ago." She grabbed the board from him. "How do you remember that?"

"I remember a lot of things."

His words were laced with the memories of long ago, and judging by the intensity of his eyes, those memories were just as real for him as they were for her. Only she wasn't naive enough to think that Marcus had spent any of the two years since they'd last seen each other lying in bed, staring up at the ceiling, and remembering exactly what it felt to lie together and feel the heat from his body wrapped around her. Not that she had. Not in months, anyway. And there was no way he needed to know that.

"Well, I hope I remember how to snowboard." She put as much flippancy into her voice as she could manage. Deanna was determined to keep the situation as light as possible. There was no need to bring any feelings or memories into play. In fact, it was probably for the best if she could just repress all of those feelings. No. It was *definitely* for the best.

"I'm sure it'll all come back to you." Marcus dropped his board to the snow and stepped in. "And there's only one way to find out." He strapped his boot into the binding, and Deanna followed suit. There was no point prolonging the torture. Besides, the sooner she got it over with, the better. "Ready?" he asked after a moment and Deanna simply nodded.

Thankfully, they were joined on the chairlift by two skiers who were visiting on a ski holiday and with it being their first trip to Stone Summit, they had plenty of questions to keep Marcus busy for the ride up the mountain. Despite the fact that she was saved from making conversation with him, Deanna was distinctly aware of his strong thigh pressed up against hers and she could feel the heat even through her thick snow pants.

"Ready for this?" Marcus looked over at her as they approached the top of the chairlift; she nodded and bit down on her bottom lip. Getting off the chair was always her least favorite part. She'd fallen one time and caused a bit of a jam-up of people, and although it had only happened once, the whole situation had been so mortifying, she always got nervous when it came to disembark. No matter how many times she'd done it successfully. "You'll be fine." He put his hand on her leg.

It was so unexpected, Deanna jerked her head up and stared at him right as their boards hit the snow-covered ramp at the top of the lift. Before she knew what was happening, Marcus took her hand to guide her off the chair and down the ramp. The entire time her board slid beneath her, all she could think of was that Marcus was touching her, and how nothing good could come from it.

The heat from her hand, even through the thick glove, singed Marcus to the core. It had been two and a half years. Long enough that the woman shouldn't have that kind of effect on him. He took a second to compose himself, thankful that Deanna wasn't looking at him. After he'd let go of her hand, she'd sat in the snow and had focused on strapping her boot into the board ever since. She definitely gave it more attention than was necessary, but he wasn't going to say anything; he needed the time to pull himself together. He knew it was a bad idea to take Deanna Gordon out snowboarding. No, it was flat out a bad idea for him to be alone with her in any capacity. And even if it didn't make any sense, and even if he knew logically that those old feelings should have burned out long ago, it was clear they hadn't. Hell, he'd only held her hand, and through a glove nonetheless. His body should not react the way it was. He shouldn't have the intense urge to grab her and pull her tight to him so she could feel for herself that his body still remembered hers.

But he couldn't. He'd lost that right a long time ago. Not that he'd even had it. Not really.

Marcus dropped down next to her in the snow and strapped his own boot into his board. "Okay." He straightened up. "Are you ready to do this?" He knew his face was a carefully composed mask. He wouldn't give anything away.

She nodded.

"Let's start on an easy run, just until it comes back to you. Sound good?"

She nodded again.

"So remember, just point your board down and relax your

body. I think you'll be surprised with how much it remembers." She still didn't say anything, but nodded her agreement. "Are you good, Dee?" He slipped easily into the use of her nickname. "You're not saying much."

She looked away and stared down over the hill. "I'm good. I got this."

He smiled and resisted the urge to reach out and touch her again. She'd always been so determined. It was one of the things that had attracted him to her in the first place. He'd never seen such a driven woman. When she set her mind to something, she went after it. It had been hot as hell back then, when she had just graduated from medical school and was home for a break, and it was even hotter now. "Then let's do this." He pushed up off the snow.

Because he was the teacher, he waited until Deanna headed down the hill. He watched as she started off shaky and unsure but in only a few turns, she settled in and carved through the snow as if it had only been a few days instead of years since she'd been on a board. He grinned and with a jump, set off down the mountain to catch up with her.

They finished the easy run with no drama and when Deanna pulled the goggles off her face onto her helmet, her broad, beautiful smile took over her face. "That was amazing. I totally remembered how to do it."

Marcus laughed. "Of course you did. Once a boarder, always a boarder. And the next one's going to be even better."

"Next one? Are we doing it again?" She clapped her gloved hands like a little girl.

"Of course. This lesson isn't over yet." He bent and freed one foot from the board and she did the same. When he stood again, he watched her for a second.

"Are you ready?" Deanna swung her head around and caught him staring at her. "What?"

He shook his head. "Nothing. Should we go?" He'd made

himself vulnerable to her once before and she'd broken his heart. He'd be dammed if he was going to let it happen again. He'd never believed in love at first sight; hell, Marcus had never believed in love. But when he met Deanna, it was instant. Their time together had been short, but it had been intense and the only real feelings he'd ever had for a woman. Not that it mattered; she'd rejected him and completely broken his heart, turning tail and returning to Toronto without so much as a second glance. As if he'd meant nothing to her. And he hadn't been able to say a word about it, because at that time, Marcus hadn't exactly been available to be with another woman, let alone fall in love with one. He'd been dating Kylie Wilson, who now happened to be happily engaged to his twin brother, Malcolm.

He wasn't proud of his past, or the fact that he'd been a terrible boyfriend to Kylie. It wasn't a secret that Marcus had cheated on Kylie—a lot—and generally treated her terribly. That was ancient history, and Kylie had long since forgiven him. But what was a secret was that one of those people he'd cheated on her with had been Deanna. No one in town knew that they'd been together, and he'd hated keeping it a secret, but not nearly as much as Deanna had. He'd known at the time it was killing her to lie to her family and friends, but he'd pushed to keep it quiet until the night he put it all on the line and told her he was in love with her and he wanted to be with her.

He was so sure she'd meet him the next day so together they could go tell Kylie the truth, and finally be free to be together. He'd been up all night planning how they could make things work together: her and her medical career, and him with his dreams to be a professional snowboarder. It seemed impossible, but he knew it wasn't. He'd never felt so full of hope and possibility—he'd been madly in love.

But she never showed up at his apartment the way they'd

planned. He'd waited for hours, called her, left messages before he finally discovered she'd left and gone back to Toronto. She never even said good-bye and he was crushed. A few days later, the offer came to join the pro snowboarding circuit, and Marcus had left town, too, vowing never to let himself be so vulnerable again. And he hadn't.

"You look like you're thinking about something," Deanna pushed. "Everything okay?"

Marcus put a smile on his face and gave her a wink. "Perfectly." He pushed his way into the chairlift line.

Whatever had happened between them, it had happened a long time ago in a complete different world and as far as he was concerned, Deanna was just another piece of ass from his past. At least that's what he was going to keep telling himself. At least until he started to believe it.

She'd managed to work all her nerves out during the first run, and Deanna was surprised how quickly boarding came back to her. More than that, she was surprised by how much she enjoyed it. The thrill of the cold air on her face as she pushed her body to perform was exhilarating.

"I forgot how awesome this was!" Deanna called behind her as she moved down the hill.

Marcus caught up to her easily and sprayed her with snow as he carved close to her and passed her.

She could only hear his laughter as he went by, and she pushed even harder to catch him although there was no way she could. But Marcus slowed, a move she knew he'd done on purpose, and they finished the run together, coming to a stop in front of the lodge.

"That was fantastic," Deanna said through deep breaths as

she tried to control her breathing. "But man, I'm out of shape."

"I think your shape looks pretty fantastic."

She snapped her head up to see his eyes glittering with mischief. After the initial sparks between them—or at least, on her end—she'd managed to compartmentalize any of her left-over feelings for Marcus and enjoy herself despite them. Not that her body wasn't completely aware of his proximity when they rode up the chair together, or when he guided her with a hand on her lower back as they made their way through the line. No, her body was totally aware of him, but the only way she knew to survive being close to Marcus was to bottle up every single one of those feelings, the same way she had years ago. And that's just what she did. So far it had worked pretty well. But that was when she'd had snowboarding to distract her. Now that they stood only inches apart, with no boards between them, Deanna suddenly wasn't so sure how to behave. What was the etiquette for such a situation?

"So," she started, "I guess I should—"

"Hey!"

They both turned at the voice. Deanna's stomach flipped while her heart soared. "Kylie?" She was going to run over to her old friend, but stopped herself only seconds before she remembered her boots were still strapped into the board. She quickly bent and released herself but by the time she had, Kylie had joined them. Deanna wrapped her friend into a bear hug. Catching up through social media and email just wasn't the same and they really hadn't had much time to chat at Kylie's party a few weeks ago—not that Deanna had made the time. She felt guilty about avoiding her, but despite the fact that it had been years since she'd betrayed her by sneaking around with Marcus, and Kylie was now happier than ever with Malcolm, the guilt had only gotten worse. She hated herself for what she'd done all those years ago; it didn't matter that Kylie had never found out. In fact, that little detail probably only made it worse.

"I thought you were gone at nursing school," Deanna said. "What are you doing here?"

Kylie laughed and looked over her shoulder at Malcolm, who just joined them. "Malcolm has an elaborate schedule that gets me back here as much as possible. I swear, it's like I never left."

"Well, I'll take it while we can." Malcolm wrapped his arm around Kylie and pulled her close. "Classes have only just started. Pretty soon my little student here will be too busy studying to come visit me."

Kylie smacked him lightly in the chest. "Stop it. I'll never be too busy for you." She gave him a sweet look that ended in a passionate kiss. Deanna glanced at Marcus, and they exchanged a quick look.

"We have to go have coffee or something," Kylie said to her when she was done smooching her fiancé. "We can steal Cynthia away, too, and get all caught up on everything. I'm so glad you're back in town."

"I'm not really back."

"Well, you're more back than I am these days." Kylie laughed. "Seriously, I feel like going to nursing school came at the worst time ever. With Cynthia's baby and now you being back, it's—"

"The perfect time." Malcolm interrupted her with a smile and a quick kiss on the forehead. "You're going to be the best nurse ever, and there would never be a good time to go away."

"It's true," Marcus chimed in. "Besides, we'll keep Malcolm plenty busy while you're away."

Kylie glanced between the two brothers and shook her head. "That's what I'm afraid of." She looked toward Deanna. "You're going to have to help me out."

"Me?" Deanna's hand flew to her chest. "How can I help you?"

"Keep this one out of trouble," she pointed to Marcus and shook her head, "and far away from my man."

"What?" Deanna took a step back. "Why would I be able to keep him out of trouble?" She didn't dare risk a glance at Marcus, afraid of what simply looking at him would give away. "I don't know any—"

Kylie's laughter cut her off. "You know how he can be."

A completely irrational fear rose up in Deanna. Kylie couldn't possibly know that of course, Deanna knew exactly how Marcus could be because he'd been that way with her. No. She couldn't know, but if she did...Deanna glanced around; the proper words for what should be a completely simple situation totally eluded her.

Ironically, Marcus saved her. "Of course she knows how I can be," he said. "Or should I say, how I used to be. A man can change, Kylie. I'm no longer the troublemaker you seem to think I am." He gave her such a charming smile, even Deanna was fooled by his words.

"You know I love you, Marcus." Kylie beamed at him. "And all that's ancient history. I'm on to bigger and better things these days."

It was much later, after Deanna and Kylie made promises to get together for coffee or drinks, and Deanna had returned her equipment and drove down the mountain to her childhood home, that Kylie's words played on repeat in her head. *That's ancient history.*

Was it? Would Kylie forgive her for betraying her friendship all those years ago when she risked everything to follow her instincts on a love that she'd ultimately walked away from?

Read the rest of Summit of Passion NOW!

About the Author

Elena Aitken is a USA Today Bestselling Author of more than forty romance and women's fiction novels. Living a stone's throw from the Rocky Mountains with her teenager twins, their two cats and a goofy rescue dog, Elena escapes into the mountains whenever life allows. She can often be found with her toes in the lake and a glass of wine in her hand, dreaming up her next book and working on her own happily ever after with her very own mountain man.

To learn more about Elena:
www.elenaaitken.com
elena@elenaaitken.com

Made in the USA
Coppell, TX
23 November 2020

41975326R00111